BLURB

Cheval is a part-time Graphic Designer and part-time Artist who uses her dreams to inspire her creativity. What happens when she finds the perfect man in her dreams? Can a woman get too much sleep when she's in the arms of a tall, dark stranger?

Morpheus is the Lord of Dreams. He's bored and lonely. He knows that his brothers Destiny and Destruction have found their happy-ever-after within the human realm. When he controls the sleeping world, can he find the one female who stands out above all others in time to save your sanity?

MORPHEUS'S DREAM

DUTIFUL GODS

BOOK THREE

MELISSA BELL

CONTENT WARNING

The following Books contains Adult (18+)
Themes, including graphic sexual scenes
and language that may offend or disturb
some readers.
All characters are fictional and portrayed as
mature adults 18 years old and over.

DEDICATION

~ Jordin Thiele ~
My rock, my mortar, my glue.

Love Always

CHAPTER 1

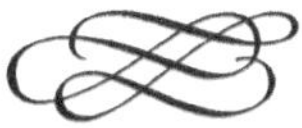

Morpheus sat in the dark. It was always dark somewhere in the human world.

As The Lord of Dreams, it was his duty to oversee the realm of sleep. He probably wouldn't have resented his duties so much, if he, himself, could sleep. Insomnia could eventually make a person go crazy and being a god was no exception. That said, who in the human world really understood what their dreams were about?

Flickered images, unknown faces, places they had never seen. He toyed with them all; he played with everyone's dreams like musical instruments. His powers enabled him to take on the form of anyone... or anything.

He often showed up as a stranger's face amongst the crowd in a dream. He could be the inspiration for many brilliant ideas, or the monster trapping you in your worst nightmare.

Some he just loved to fuck around with, making them dream of flying pink elephants with purple spots. For others, he brought to life their deepest fears in the darkness of sleep.

What he wouldn't give to be able to close his own eyes and sink into a dreamless state of rest. He was immune to his own sand, the precious dream dust that crowned him 'Sandy,' short for 'Sandman,' by his siblings.

The dreams he'd manipulated lately were getting more senseless and bent out of shape than ever. Some resembled a three car pile-up.

He was becoming more and more unsettled, erratic within his role. He felt like an over-stretched rubber band, worn thin, about to snap. He couldn't keep going like this; his appearance was even beginning to take on a reckless, unkempt persona. His five o'clock shadow had become the norm along with his messy curls.

He spun the large globe of the earth, took a small dose of sand in his palm, and as it spun, he blew the sand across its surface, spreading it far and wide with his breath. Then, he waited.

He leaned back into his chair, closed his tired eyes, as he began to watch various images passed through his mind. He plucked one and brought it forward for closer inspection. It was Claire's dream, a little girl aged six. She wanted to know what it was like to ride a pony. Claire had been injured in a car accident when she was three. She would never walk again. He indulged the wishes of the little girl by giving her what she wanted most. He appeared in her dream as a small white pony. He knelt down for her to climb on his back. The colors around them were vibrant. He walked at first, allowing her to get used to the sway and moment. In her dream, she could walk and run like all the other kids. Her joyous laughter spurred him on. They trotted for a bit before he turned and cantered home. He bent down again allowing her to dismount easily. Claire stepped up to his nose and planted a big kiss, "Thank you, this is the best day I've ever had." She patted him for a moment before he allowed the dream to fade into the back of his mind. He had not lost his empathy for children.

He opened his eyes and took a sip of water from the glass next to him. Pity he couldn't die, thinking to himself. He would have checked out of this shit a long time ago.

He saw another image that bothered him. He pulled and unfolded it before he went to work. This time it was Stephanie, a mother of three; she was thinking about going back to her abusive husband. He couldn't help but remind her of why she had left him in the first place and how it wasn't safe for her or her kids if she went back. He needed to show her how great things could be if she stayed on the path she had taken.

He appeared as a thirty year old blond man, dressed in a tuxedo. A single, long-stemmed rose in his hand. She answered his knock. He artistically painted her dream, as he wined her, dined her and showed her that the right man could open the doors to a whole new life for her and her children.

He stood at her front door, took her in his arms, and leaned in to kiss her good night as the dream faded away.

CHEVAL HAD BEEN COMMISSIONED TO DESIGN the new menus for a restaurant opening in a week. Gerry, the owner and head chef, was making her job harder by changing the details of the opening night menu. That made four fucking times in the last week. He'd changed the cover, the color, the print, and the various meals to be listed. His constant demands had her putting other work on hold. She smiled to herself and thought, 'fingers crossed he approves this draft,' as she hit the send key.

She was an artist at heart, but she took commission work in between gallery exhibits. She placed her head down on the table to wait for Gerry's response.

She must have nodded off. She was watching a tall dark haired man. He was sitting in a throne-like chair. The room he sat in was dark. He wore black leather pants and displayed a washboard upper torso. His eyes were closed, and his face was tortured, as though he was caught in a bad dream. Beside him was a large globe of earth, and in his hand, he held a drawstring pouch. He was magnificent, even with his brows pulled tightly together like he was in pain. She took a step closer, unbelievably drawn to him. His eyes snapped open, she let out a squeak and sat bold upright in front of her computer. The in-box flashing 'you have mail.' She closed her eyes for a second to let her mind photograph the image she had just dreamed.

Her next gallery exhibition was a few weeks away, and she had found her focus, her muse. She didn't care if a male could be titled a muse, she would make him a star.

Reading Gerry's response, she breathed a huge sigh of relief. He was finally happy with the design and layout; he asked to have it sent to print. She forwarded the file on to

Carolyn at Images Ink. She planned to drop by in the morning to pick them up. Finally finished with Gerry's project, she moved on to the front window design for her friend Harley's tattoo studio. She grabbed her sketchpad and pencil, and poured herself a glass of wine, before relocating onto the couch to start her drawing.

She lost herself within her sketches. Reaching for her glass and lifting it to her lips, she took a sip, and then turned back to the pad on her lap. 'What the fuck?' The man from her dreams was staring back at her from the page.

CHAPTER 2

Morpheus stood slowly from his seat, he was confused and disorientated. He looked around his library, but he was alone. The woman with the dark brown hair and chocolate-colored eyes was gone. In his current state of mind, he couldn't determine if she had really been standing in front of him, or if he'd imagined her. It was as if she'd looked at him rather than through him. He'd sensed someone watching him. He sat back down and quickly closed his eyes. He searched every corner of his mind, and eventually he gave up. She must be awake. He wouldn't be able to find her unless she slept. Disgruntled, he decided to wipe everyone's dreams to wait for the dark beauty to fall back to sleep.

After waiting for what felt like hours (but in reality was only minutes), he decided to go and find something to eat. His sister Faith had left a variety of edibles. He could only remember eating the last time she stocked up his fridge. Time seemed irrelevant to him, he had no concept of day or night, time, date or year. All he knew was if he closed his eyes, there were always people dreaming. Once upon a time, he actually gave a shit, but now he couldn't care less, except for the brown-haired beauty. He would give anything to see her again, to see what she dreamed about. He found himself wondering, did she have a boyfriend or husband? It wouldn't matter, he'd make her his in her dreams. He pulled a chocolate crème brûlée from the fridge; the chocolate and sugar would add a little buzz to his dream manipulation. He laughed to himself; his sister knew his sweet tooth so well. He took a spoon from the drawer and sat on a stool at the kitchen bench, closing his eyes while he ate. He didn't want to lose the opportunity to see her again.

CHEVI THREW HER SKETCHPAD AND PENCIL on the couch beside her and downed the remnants of her glass in one go. What the fuck? She was tired but too hyped up to sleep. With a sigh, she stood with her hands on her hips, she needed to unwind enough to go to bed and crash. Her mind was obviously focused on something other than the required design of a shop window. She carried the glass to the kitchen and placed it in the sink and headed to her studio. She lived in a two-bedroom apartment. It definitely wasn't the Hilton, but certainly no hovel either. It was affordable. Sure it could be nicer, but one day she hoped to upgrade, one day when she was rich and famous. She laughed to herself, 'Yeah, but artists have to die before they get true recognition.' With that thought she looked at the clock on the wall, 10:30pm. Too late to ring and see how her mother was doing. They'd lost her father to a heart attack a couple of months earlier and her mother was packing up his things this weekend. She'd asked her to come home and help clear out the garage. She smiled. Her mother was going to make it into a sewing room. Chevi figured it was a good use of space, but didn't know if she could bring herself to go through her father's things, not yet anyway. She'd work it out tomorrow.

She stood inside the door of the spare room she'd christened her art studio. It was crammed with canvases of various sizes leaning against the walls. Out of the corner of her eye, she spied the perfect one. She lifted the huge frame to her easel and adjusted its height. The canvas was almost as tall as her shoulder. She readied her supplies, closed her eyes and visualized the scene. She dipped her brush and began to mark-up the outline. She lost herself in her painted dreamscape.

The desperate need to pee brought her back from her trance. She downed her tools and raced for the toilet. As she washed her hands, she glanced over her appearance.

Damn, she needed to find time to do something with her hair. Under closer scrutiny, she shook her head, her eyebrows had gone native. Maybe tomorrow she would have a pamper day, she thought, as she removed her clothes. After switching off the lights, she turned to the comfort of her bed. She could hear the cool thousand weave sheets calling her name.

She set her alarm, it was currently 1:00am, and she had to be up early to catch up on her workload. She pulled the sheet, with exhaustion she closed her eyes and gave in, quickly falling asleep.

CHAPTER 3

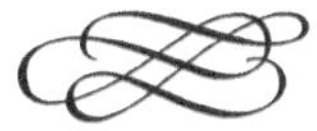

Morpheus left the kitchen after he'd consumed three parfaits. He savoured the indulgence of the creamy goo. He hadn't been this eager to see anyone in a really long time. He kept his eyes closed while he showered and dried off. The excitement of seeing her again on top of all that sugar had him twitching. He lay down naked on his king-sized bed and placed his hands behind his head. Again, he waited.

He had all but given up and knew he should return to his normal havoc in the dreamworld, but he couldn't. His body was so wired, his cock had hardened in anticipation. Was that all it was, a sexual attraction?

He'd had those in the past. 'No!' he told himself. The brown-haired female was different. He was sure that she'd seen him, truly looked at him. He wasn't certain how she did it, but he'd investigate it later, just not now.

CHEVI WAS SEARCHING FOR SOMETHING... someone. She was in that dark room again with the giant throne and globe, but the chair was empty. She turned in a circle to find him, but he wasn't there. She spied a door, a little anxious about what she might find on the other side, but she needed to know, anyway. She'd always been one to overcome her fears. She exited the room into a hallway. Looking both ways, she saw another door. It was open a crack. 'Well,' she thought, 'that's an open invitation.' She quietly pushed it open with one finger, prying around it tentatively. Chevi sucked in a deep breath. It was him, the man of her dreams. He was in a bedroom, laid out naked, as if he was waiting for a lover. Surveying the room, she established that nobody else was there. She stepped to the side of the massive bed and looked at him with the eyes of an artist. She exhaled the breath she hadn't realized she'd been holding. His black hair so dark it resembled the color of a crow's feather. His eyes shadowed, the word 'weary' came to mind. His lips looked like they tasted of days, the kind you could lose yourself in with just one kiss. His strong jawline described a man that was ruggedly handsome. Her eyes travelled along his arm tucked behind his head. She wondered what it would be like to be wrapped up in such strength. She continued her appreciation of this spectacular specimen of a man. Down his neck past his solid chest and to his toned abdomen. She glanced back at his face. He appeared to be sleeping, so she returned her observation to trail lower. My god, he had those side muscle things in front of his hips. His legs were well-defined muscle, like he worked out in a gym. The man even had sexy feet, what the fuck was that about? Her eyes were drawn back to the hardening ridge of his cock. She felt a spike of jealousy for the woman he was dreaming of. Her fingers itched to touch him, to circle his dick with her hand. It twitched, a bead of pre-cum seeped out of the slit, she licked her lips.

She felt her pussy ache to life, throbbing to know what he would feel like inside her, his large girth stretching her walls. Her breathing became ragged, temptation too much, her hand snuck out. Chevi's thumb brushed over the bead, collecting a sample. She lifted it to her lips, her tongue taking a taste, she moaned..... Her alarm went off. She slammed her hand down on the snooze. FUCK!

Morpheus opened his eyes and smiled, followed by a frown. She was fucking beautiful, his female was gorgeous, she was different, special. She was his. He would do everything in his power to have her.

His body ached, to feel her hands on him, her lips. Unable to ignore the throb in his groin, he lowered his hand to smear the moisture over the head of his cock. He circled himself, playing back in his mind the way she had looked at him, as he stroked himself. He wondered if she would have taken him with those luscious lips. Her tongue swirling around his crown. His grip increased and his strokes took on a quicker, more desperate rhythm. His hips lifted off the bed as the base of his cock signaled his cum working up his shaft. He growled as his cum exploded into the air. He would give his soul to be inside that warm wet mouth. Hot pulses of seed landed on his chest.

CHEVAL WATCHED ON AS HE PLEASURED himself, her pussy weeping, crying for his thickness. Her lips tingled to be kissed by his cock. She wanted to taste more of his essence as his release painted his torso. Her pussy ached and throbbed for its own attention. She was interrupted in thought by that incessant alarm going off... again. She moaned, rolled over, and grabbed the clock from the bedside table. She pitched it across the room. Three minutes later as it still blared from the battery backup, she climbed out of bed begrudgingly and then ripped its guts out, and tossed it on the bed. "Fucking piece of shit!" She would have thrown the bastard in the bin, except she needed it.

CHAPTER 4

As she stepped into the shower, her nipples were so tightly puckered they hurt. Her pussy was throbbing with need. The rivulets of water running down over her sensitized flesh as she rinsed the conditioner out of her hair made her think about her dream man. She couldn't ignore her body's demand any longer. She braced her back against the tiled wall and closed her eyes as she started to daydream about his hands cupping her lust heavy breasts. She pictured him as his tongue circled her nipples, first one, and then the other. Her hand settled between her legs, with her fingers dancing around her swollen clit. Her legs began to shake as her pussy tightened, grasping for something solid. She imagined him filling her with a hard thrust, forcing her to cum for him. Her heart raced, she cried out as her orgasm surged, her pussy contracting around her fingers as she drove them inside, ringing out every spasm. The butt of her hand kissed her needy button with every stroke.

Breathing heavily, she collected herself enough to finish her shower. Dressed in a well-worn pair of jeans and T-shirt, she quickly checked her emails. She had to get to the print shop, pick up the menus and then drop them off at Gerry's so she could collect her check.

After that she had to get her ass home and work on the designs that had been shelved. Once all that was done, she was free to get lost in her own paintings.

MORPHEUS HAD NO IDEA WHERE TO START looking for information. He'd thought about asking his mother, but quickly changed his mind when he considered her biting his head off for not maintaining his duties and losing focus. Not like she cared, she very rarely came to visit.

Not wanting her to pick up on his thoughts, he stopped thinking about her. He didn't want her popping in for an untimely visit.

If he had a name, he could search Destiny's library. What the hell was he going to do during her waking hours?

He closed his eyes, reluctantly ready to resume his duties when he saw his brown-haired beauty. The vision was cloudy, like he was seeing through fog. She was in the shower, with him; his tongue was licking and teasing her cherry colored nipples. His hand between her legs, as he lifted her, she locked her ankles at his back. He watched as he pushed his cock inside her with one hard stroke. That was all she needed, she came riding out her orgasm. Her head fell forward on his shoulder as her breathing slowed. The vision faded away, leaving him less than satisfied.

He was screwed, his eyes flew open.

Fuck! He jumped out of bed. He needed to get this shit sorted. He headed for a shower, a cold one. He needed it if he was going to use his brain. He knew there was something different, something intriguing about his brown-haired beauty. He just needed to work out what that was. She didn't only see him in her dreams while she slept, she saw him in her daydreams as well. She had the ability to manipulate him into the dream, draw him in, and recognize him in his own form.

If his suspicions were right, then he could make her his female. He vaguely re-called his mother showing him some text in an ancient book.

He quickly showered and threw on some sweat pants before heading to his library. He needed to find that book.

Chevi stopped at the bank to deposit the check for her work on the menus. While waiting in line for the teller to call her forward, she felt a tap on her shoulder. She turned slightly to see Olivia, her friend and owner of the gallery that would be organizing the show of her latest collection. Liv greeted her with a smile, "How's everything coming along for the exhibition?"

She wasn't about to let on that her direction had changed drastically from a week ago. She still had three weeks left to prepare all the pieces in time. 'Fingers crossed' she thought. "Everything's going really well, right on schedule."

Chevi knew if she could get the rest of her commission work out of the way, it would leave her to pull as many all-nighters as she needed. She'd done it before, she could do it again.

The teller called, "Next." She quickly moved to the window and made her deposit. As she left, she waved at Liv, who gave her the universal sign for 'call me.'

She arrived home in time to quickly read her emails and make a cup of coffee before settling into her next project. She had to finish the shop front window design for the tattoo shop.

On her third attempt, she felt like she'd

hit gold. She drew the upper body of a man standing straight on with tattoos, and a curvaceous woman showing a full back job. To the side of the couple, she wrote in decorative script 'Get Inked'. Satisfied with the way it had come together, she went to work on her computer to fine tune the image, before sending it off for approval to her friend, Harley. She'd been thinking about getting another tattoo herself. She too was a collector, her back was full. She had various ones scattered in places that were easily covered to uphold a professional appearance in the business world. You would think that in today's society, people would be able to see past the stigma, and be more tolerant, but sadly it wasn't the case. If only she could afford to be a full-time artist, it wouldn't matter what people thought.

She felt a sense of accomplishment as she moved on to the invitations for the gallery showing.

She decided to call it 'Dreams & Nightmares.' She moved the mouse over the screen until she had the script right, then chose a background. She completed the date and time of the exhibition, then picked up the phone to call Olivia. "Hi Liv, it's Chevi. You asked me to call, I'm just ringing to confirm the invitations are done, how many invites would you like printed?"

Olivia replied, "Shoot for the stars, I'm thinking a hundred. How soon can you get them to me?"

"Well, if you'd like to send a guest list over to the printers, I'll send the print file and they will take care of the rest. Carolyn owes me a favor and has offered to help out."

"Sounds wonderful. Can you send me the email address to send the list too? I'll get straight on it today." she gushed, before hanging up.

Chevi copied the email address into a text and sent it off for Liv to take care of her side of things.

CHAPTER 5

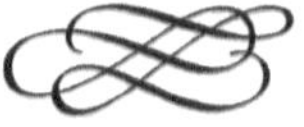

After making a modest chicken salad for lunch, Chevi migrated to her studio. She put on some music and became entranced with her painting. Her hips swayed to the music as she filled the canvas with the picture from her mind. She imagined what it might be like to be held in the strong hands, and muscular arms of the man in her painting.

She finished the final brush strokes around his closed eyes, then stepped sideways to the table to place her brushes in solvent to soak while she went and had a shower. She still had hours of work ahead of her but her shoulders, back, and neck had started to ache a while ago. The hot water and a bit of a break would hopefully give her body a second wind.

Chevi stood under the steaming hot water until she felt her tired limbs give in and the knotted muscles relax. She got out of the shower, dressed in some comfy sweats and a t-shirt. She didn't bother with putting on underwear. She didn't want to feel restricted or confined.

She hummed to herself as she went to the kitchen and made a cup of coffee, then took a sip so as not to spill it on the way back to her studio. Her grip on the handle loosened enough to tip hot coffee on her toes as she entered the studio and looked at her painting. 'What the fuck? What the fuck?' She put her cup down on the table and looked around the small room. The brushes she'd used to paint were still sitting in the jar of solvent. She was confused, beyond confused actually. She checked over her shoulder to the empty hall. Her reality wavered, she was sure she'd painted him with his closed eyes, now they were open and they had that uncanny ability, that no matter where you stood, they appeared to be looking straight at you. A shiver went down her spine and she broke into a sweat. Not again! Not now! She hadn't had an episode in more than ten years. She kept shaking her head frantically from side to side as she began to cry.

Chevi backed out of the room, no longer able to tell what was real, and what was a dream. Her worlds had collided, she had no one she could talk to, and her mother would think she was in the midst of a breakdown or worse, going crazy again.

She couldn't go back there, nobody would understand, she barely made it to sixteen in that place. Her parents had put her in a hospital for loonies. That's what all the kids she went to school with used to say, 'The Loony Bin.'

Chevi had been a normal child, she'd talked and played with imaginary friends like most other kids her age, but her parents often berated her about her made up stories and embellished tales. They said she had an over-active imagination. That she dreamed so vividly, she couldn't tell what was real and what was all in her head.

The doctors kept her locked up for nearly a year until she was so medicated she no longer dreamt at all.

When she was first admitted, before they'd subjected her to so many drugs, she was often found wandering the halls in the middle of the night. At first, they'd only put her in a padded room, and locked the door, but after they discovered her walking around outside her room so many times after lights out, they'd resorted to restraining her. She'd hated the place bad enough, but to tie her down to her bed left her feeling vulnerable and resentful. She'd seen movies and watched the news that told stories about places like these, it made her feel uneasy. Yet, even restrained, she was still able to escape. The final stage to stop her from playing Houdini was to sedate her so heavily she no longer saw the beautiful scenes behind her closed lids. She felt like a zombie and resembled one as well in her hospital-issue gown. She no longer cared about anything, she lost her passion for art, laughter and breath.

So heavily medicated, she hadn't even registered a change in surroundings when they put her into the general population ward. She could still remember that horrible taste in the back of her throat even at the memory of the medication. She could still feel the zingy sensation in her fillings. Who knew what the hell that shit was about? But she didn't like it, her hand went to her head and her knees buckled and everything went black.

She was floating, disoriented, like an out-of-body experience. Reluctant to open her eyes in case she was back in the place of her nightmares, she kept her lids closed.

Her back met with the softness of a mattress, she held her breath. Still she resisted the urge to open her eyes until smooth flesh was pressed to her lips. The tip of her tongue darted out of her mouth and made contact. She opened her eyes at the sound of a sharp intake of breath, followed by a mumbled curse.

MORPHEUS KNEW THE SECOND HIS FEMALE'S eyes had closed, and she'd lost consciousness. He pounced into action. He was right there with her in the black void between his realm and the nightmare that began to take on a smoky haze in the corner of her mind.

Nightmares always looked like a fire without a flame. Smoke billowed until the entire space was filled, and from within the haze walked fear. Morpheus sucked air into his lungs with a long drawn inhale and consumed it all. He would study it later when he had time to dissect it properly. For now, he would protect his female the only way he knew how. He would keep her safe in her sleep. Her heart raced and her muscles twitched in her unconscious state, like she was readying herself for an invisible battle.

He lifted her into his arms and carried her to his bed. He gently laid her down. His eyes became riveted on the fullness of her lips, unaware that his thumb had been drawn to them. He licked his own lips with want, and the need to feel hers pressed against his. 'Fuck' he thought. He'd never wanted a woman so much in his long lifetime. This female was his though, and he planned to keep her. He drew in a sharp breath before he moaned and growled, as the wet tip of her tongue peaked out and made contact with his skin, his cock instantly stiffened with desire. He watched her eyelids flutter open and her cheeks flushed. She appeared to be holding her breath.

He raised one eyebrow and said, "Hi."

Chevi opened her eyes to see the man of her dreams and exhaled with relief. She wasn't where she thought she would end up.

His voice made her skin tingle as though every nerve ending zinged with energy. She knew this was a dream, and in her dreams, anything was possible. She lifted herself up on her elbows to trail her tongue along his thumb. She ran it around the tip and nipped at it.

Chevi replied, "Hi," and smiled.

Morpheus was entranced by the sight of his beautiful female's playful tease. His cock throbbed at the sight of her delectable tongue and her lips' suggestive show.

He allowed her to weave her own fantasy, knowing it was wrong, but like a moth to a flame, he was powerless to do anything but fly straight into her fire.

His hand trailed down to her shoulder and slid her silky lengths back to expose the column of her neck.

"So Angel, what are we doing here?" he asked, with a heated look that ran from her eyes down to her toes and back up again.

"Anything I want, it's my dream after all," she replied, as she made his clothes disintegrate.

Dream stood there in all his proud naked glory, stunned at first that his female possessed the power to accomplish such a task. It spurred his ego to know he had found someone he could call his equal. He retaliated with the wave of his hand and left her in the same manner. He watched her surprised reaction bloom, "Hey!" she gasped, then giggled. If this wasn't a dream, she would have been horrified.

She continued with her seductive tease. In a dream, she could be whoever she wanted, do whatever she wanted and not have to hide from her needs as a woman.

In real life, she would never be this open, flirtatious or wanton. She lost all of her inhibitions, along with her insecurities.

Morpheus thought she was exquisite, her skin flawless, he wanted to trace every mark on her skin with his tongue to see if it tasted as rich as the colors they simulated.

Not wanting to waste a minute of time in this dream, Chevi crooked her index finger and curled it to call him nearer. She rose on her elbows to meet him half way. As his mouth drew closer, her heart beat quickened.

Morpheus brushed his lips against hers, a burst of music infiltrated the room, and his female vanished.

CHAPTER 6

Chevi woke to the ring tone of her mobile phone. The last thing she remembered was a dream. "Aargh!" She punched the floor, it had happened again. Just when she'd been about to get to know her dream man intimately. The hit was absorbed by the softness of her quilt-covered mattress. She'd lost her grip on reality. 'What the fuck? How did I get here?' Puzzled, she shivered as a breeze flowed through the open bedroom window she had forgotten to close. The weather had taken on a coolness to the afternoons that made for cold nights. Suddenly chilled, she sat bolt upright on her bed, and looked down at herself as her phone on the bedside table started to ring again, 'Why am I naked? Where the hell are my clothes?' she mumbled, confused.

She let the call go to message bank. If it was important, they'd leave a message. She wasn't up to speaking to anyone right now.

Her stomach growled as she looked around for her t-shirt and pants. "Wait a second," she said to herself. She ran over the fractured memories, to figure out what had happened.

She remembered having a shower, getting dressed, making coffee, and then her mental hardware zapped her with the image of the altered picture. She thought about her reaction and identified it as a panic attack, she remembered everything going black, and concluded she must have hyperventilated until she passed out.

She hated the sense of being unstable, the constant need to confirm reality. Chevi knew her art would suffer if she spoke to her doctor and was put back on medication again.

It made her brain too fuzzy to think

clearly, her imagination too hazy to focus and her attitude too complacent and lazy to create.

At least her dreams were of a sex god, with electrically charged lips. She unconsciously lifted her hand to her lips. They still tingled. She wondered if men like that really existed, or if her sex-deprived brain had a knack for dreaming up the impossible.

She tried to remember the last time she'd actually had sex, or even had a regular date. It felt as if it had been forever. It was strange how time flew when life happened. She breathed a heavy-hearted sigh. She needed to get out more, and work didn't count. Maybe she'd think about all that after the exhibition. In order to pay the bills and have some spare change, she'd have to sell most, if not all, of her collection, which at the moment only consisted of just one piece. She gathered herself and searched around for her missing clothes. Unable to find them, she found a new set in the drawers. Dressed in her fresh set of clothes, Chevi went to the kitchen and took a nectarine from the fruit basket and a can of diet soda from the fridge, before she made her way back to the studio room. She placed her food and drink down on the table and held her breath as she turned to face the painting currently standing on the easel. With a critical eye, she inspected the entire canvas. As a perfectionist, she needed to know there weren't any recognizable flaws before she moved on to her next creation. She was determined not to focus on the fact that she was certain she'd had painted him with his closed eyes.

Chevi could feel the eyes of her dream lover follow her every move. She was proud that she'd managed to capture such a lifelike image from her imagination and transfer it through her brush strokes onto a blank canvas to obliterate the white background.

Satisfied that her work on this piece was complete, she relocated her stool so her back was against the wall. She opened her can of soda and took a couple of sips before she returned it to the table and picked up the ripe nectarine. She rolled it round in her hand as she looked at the amazing colors of the skin. She'd bought half a dozen of them a few days ago and this was the last one she had left. She didn't know why, but she'd always had a fixation with stone fruit; nectarines, peaches, and cherries. Not so much apricots; they played up with her digestion a little too much, but she rarely bought anything other fruit.

She closed her eyes as her teeth sank through the skin into the soft sweet flesh of the fruit. She moaned. There'd always been something erotic about it. The flavor hit her tongue and behind her closed lids, she pictured her dream lover.

MORPHEUS'S HANDS CLENCHED THE PILLOW either side of where his female's head had been. He'd leant down to brush his lip against hers. He'd been about to deepen the kiss when she was taken from him again. He'd been so distracted in the moment that he neglected to get her name. He chastised himself, 'think with your head idiot,' he glanced down at his nakedness and added 'your other head, you dick.'

He waved his hand and his pants reappeared on his body. His head had begun to feel like it was about to split in two. He couldn't hold off his duties any longer. He felt bitter about it. He could easily lose himself when it came to spending time with his female.

He had long since run out of patience, his agitation had grown too high to contain. He stretched his neck to the left then the right, clicking his neck as he walked through the door to his library. Staring at his throne, he interlocked his fingers, turned his palms away from his body and cracked his joints. He knew what he was chasing; he was looking for someone he could make pay. He was no longer the calm, thoughtful, sympathetic Dream. His mood was vicious and vindictive. His intention was to be someone's worst nightmare. Right now, he was a hunter. He moved behind his desk, his eyes closed as he planted his ass on the seat. His hands settled with white knuckles on the arm rests.

Morpheus flew through the darkness of his mind searching for the ideal candidate to release his pent up energy on. He almost missed it, but like a flash, he caught a glimpse of his woman. Someone was dreaming about her, the atmosphere was devious and malicious. He was furious...'Perfect.'

Andrew's sick and twisted mind was dreaming of watching Morpheus's female. He was dreaming of taking her mail, and climbing through an open window to her bedroom, seeing the woman that had rejected every one of his advances, dinner offers, flowers and chocolates that he'd had delivered, and how he'd found them in her trash bag. He was going to make sure she noticed him at long last. She was naked on her bed, asleep. He crept in and took her discarded clothes, lifted them to his nose and inhaled. Morpheus watched on, disgusted at what he was seeing. He observed as Andrew climbed back out the window, taking her clothes with him. He paused on the fire escape, tore the garments into shreds then re-entered the bedroom, his intentions clearly marked his face. He planned to act out his hatred.

Dream stepped out of the corner of the room, intent on stopping Andrew in his tracks. Andrew saw a huge guy move towards him, "Who the fuck are you?" he asked. "What are you doing here?"

Dream smiled crookedly at Andrew and replied, "I'm the brother of Death."

Morpheus blackened out the room, his face glowed as he opened his mouth and Andrew was swarmed with wasps that stung his face and neck over and over. His allergy to wasps kicked in and his throat swelled, blocking off his air supply. He dropped to his knees, then fell landing face down, not moving. His screams had stopped long ago, and soon, so would the beat of his heart.

Morpheus had used an incredible amount of his energy to pull off his vendetta. He faded from the dream leaving Andrew bleeding from the ears, nose and mouth. He knew there would be no escape for Andrew now. His brother would come for him soon enough, but till then, he would remain trapped inside his own nightmare

Morpheus opened his eyes and reached for the bottle of scotch. He took three long swallows, then replaced it back in the drawer.

CHAPTER 7

Chevi sat up on her stool. After staring at her dream man for a minute or two, she stood and moved the canvas off the easel. Out of the corner of her eye, she spotted the perfect size canvas for her next piece.

She imagined a dark background with an over stretched mouth spewing forth a swarm of wasps. It was a masculine mouth attached to a strong jaw. She looked over to the finished canvas. It was the jawline of her dream man.

Chevi shrugged her shoulder and went to work, outlining the image roughly. Then she blended the colors to form texture. Because she wanted this piece to appear three dimensional, she would have to set it aside to dry enough to layer the construction of it.

Several hours later, she was reminded how long she'd been at it when her stomach growled. She downed tools and wandered to the kitchen barefoot. After a quick glance in the fridge and freezer, she decided to satisfy her craving for some Chinese food. She searched for her purse and slipped her feet into her flip-flops. She snatched up her keys and headed for the door.

As she left her apartment, she ran into paramedics as they rushed by. Her neighbor Andrew was being wheeled through the courtyard, an air bag attached to his throat. She heard the paramedic say, "We're losing him."

She stood there stunned, her feet frozen on the spot. Andrew had been her neighbor for the past six months. He was kind of creepy, and followed her around, often harassing her to go out with him. He wasn't an ugly guy, but the way he watched and looked at her made her skin crawl, so she'd politely made several excuses to avoid his constant advances.

The wheels made an eerie sound on the courtyard's uneven paving. When she raised her eyes, Andrew's sister, Elaine, was watching her. There was something seriously fucked up with that family.

Elaine called out from beside her brother, "What did you do to him? You bitch! This is your fault!"

Dumbfounded, Chevi watched on as they loaded Andrew into the back of the ambulance. His sister climbed in after him as the paramedic closed the door behind them and raced to the driver's side of the vehicle.

She continued to stand there long after the ambulance had switched on its lights and siren and sped off. She listened as the sound faded away into the night traffic.

She looked over to Andrew's apartment. In the haste to get Andrew to the hospital, his front door had been left open and his lights were still on.

Without a second thought, she crossed the courtyard and went inside. The layout was the same as her own. Familiar with the location of the light switches, she made her way to the back rooms to switch them off. Systematically, she moved from one room to the next, thinking damn the place was lit up like a Christmas tree. Finally she turned to leave, but a glow from under the second bedroom door caught her eye and caused her to pause. It was the amber hue of candlelight. She ventured to the guest room, opened the door and was horrified to see an entire wall covered in pictures of her. Some were of her crossing the street, others were of her in her bedroom, bathroom and even one or two from above her bed as she satisfied herself.

At first she'd felt sorry for Andrew being taken in the ambulance, then she experienced anger and finally, she secretly hoped the bastard didn't come back. If he made it, she would have to notify the police and take out a restraining order. She would have to start thinking about some place safe to move to; his violation of her privacy was criminal. It meant he had a camera hidden in her apartment, somewhere above her bed or that he had access to the ceiling cavity.

She took her phone from her pocket and snapped pictures of the collages as well as a weird shrine-like altar he had set up in front of it. She didn't even know what half the shit on it was exactly but she knew she never wanted to see it again, considering all the objects looked like instruments you would find in a BDSM dungeon. She blew out the candles and backed out of the room feeling sick to her stomach at the thought of what Andrew was probably capable of and relieved she had listened to her intuition and refused his advances.

She left Andrew's place, and even though she was no longer hungry, she walked to the Chinese takeout not far from her place to try to get her head around what she'd just seen.

She was greeted by Frank, the owner of 'Hong's Asian Infusion', born in Sussex, England. His parents had moved to the area for a better life when he was still in primary school. The fact he was a small middle-aged

Asian man with a name like Frank always amused her.

He smiled as he took her order and repeated it back to her. "Fried Rice, Honey Duck, and Prawn Chips. It'll be about twenty minutes." He poured her a cup of green tea while she waited.

She thanked him and sat down. She used the time to catch up on her emails as she drank her tea.

Twenty minutes later, Frank walked up to where she sat, he placed the order on the table next to her and lifted the empty cup. He sat it in the palm of his hand and turned it three times before saying, "Your fortune lies within your dreams."

She refrained from letting out her first response of 'Fuck off,' and settled for the second one, "Well Frank, if I dream of the winning lottery numbers, I'll be sure to buy a ticket." She smiled, paid for her food and left to walk home.

~

DEATH MATERIALIZED IN THE ROOM OF Andrew Lewis; the guy's time was up. He rolled his eyes. Death really hated the process of claiming the ones hooked to respirators; it made it harder to suck their souls out. With a sigh, he walked to the wall, leaned back, and switched the machines off. Then he waited. After several minutes had passed, he turned them back on, the heart monitor flat- lined, sending off alarms. The room filled with nurses and doctors. Vanessa's shift had started ten minutes earlier and already she was in the middle of yet another one of those days. She raced into the room and lowered the bed to start CPR on the crashing patient. As she started chest compressions, she looked up to the empty space where Death stood observing as she began to count. A familiar shiver ran down her spine and she knew no amount of intervention was going to save this patient, but by law she'd started the resuscitation and only a doctor could release her by pronouncing a time of death.

"Why can't you leave me alone? I wish you'd stop following me," she whispered towards where the plug was now hanging half out of the wall.

Death moved to stand behind Vanessa. He leaned over her small frame, his hands rested on her hips, as he whispered into her ear, "Why do you keep fighting me? I wish you'd stop running from me." He would have put the thought straight into her head if she didn't have so many protective barriers in place.

Vanessa's body betrayed her; she bit down on her lower lip to avoid making a sound. She startled as another nurse and a doctor entered the room.

The doctor leaned over and checked for a pulse, his eyes flicked to his watch as he stepped back, "Time of death, 9:17pm, Nurse, you can stop now." He moved to the foot of the bed and continued, "His sister is down as emergency contact, I'll let her know. Would you prepare the body for her?" He moved closer to Vanessa than Death was comfortable with. He didn't like the way the doctor looked at her like she was his next conquest. The doctor suddenly felt like he couldn't breathe. A cold band around his throat cut off his air supply. He stumbled backwards away from Vanessa and dug into his coat pocket to remove an asthma puffer. As he fumbled it, it hit the floor. Vanessa made a step closer to the struggling doctor, but ran up against a force field, she noticed the other nurse move in to help the choking man, as she heard a low growl behind her. Nurse Tracy helped the doctor to retrieve his inhaler and administered a couple of doses before helping him to leave the room.

Vanessa was horrified at the scene. She had never witnessed anything like it before.

She went to the adjoining bathroom and threw up. She smoothed her uniform and rinsed her mouth, then returned to the room and resumed her duties.

She removed the intravenous drips, and the ventilator tubes, then reached down to switch the power off and noticed that the plugs were half out of their sockets.

She detached the tubing from the machines and wheeled them out of the room. She placed all the dismantled pieces into the bio-hazard bins. Her head was tripping, her emotions wrecked, she approached the nurses' station. Vanessa found the Duty Nurse and resigned, effective immediately. She raced to the locker room, took her bag out of the locker, threw her padlock and key into her bag and left.

DEATH STEPPED FORWARD, OPENED ANDREW'S mouth and inhaled a steady breath, sucking his soul from inside the dead shell. He had no warning as Andrew's last moments of his life flashed through his mind. He saw his brother Morpheus standing before him. Thousands of wasps spewing from his open mouth, he felt Andrew's bitterness twist in his stomach. His brother had circumvented this guy's death, he would have to have a word with him, but first he wanted to speak to Vanessa.

He solidified, before he went to find her. He walked to the nurses' station and said to Nurse Tracy, "Hi, I'm looking for Nurse Vanessa, can you help me?"

Tracy put a chart that she'd been making

notes in down on the bench in front of her and leaned closer, "She's not here, can I help you with something sir?" She eyed him curiously.

"No I'm a personal friend. I was in the area and thought I'd say hi." He sighed.

She leaned even closer to whisper, "She resigned, just now effective immediately. You might catch her in the car park if you hurry."

Death winked at her, "Thanks." He took off at a run towards the room he'd come from. Once inside, he vanished.

CHAPTER 8

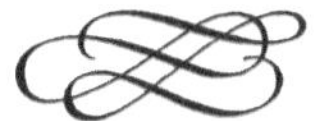

Dream sat on his throne. His body ached, his head hurt, and he felt sick. It had been forever since he'd wielded that kind of power. His muscles twitched. He hated the sensation more than ever because he wasn't able to simply climb into bed and sleep it off. His body would be like this for hours unless he slept.

He withdrew the bottle of scotch from his desk drawer and put both his feet up on the desk.

Chevi finished eating her Chinese food, closed the lids and placed the leftovers in the fridge. She yawned. The sun had gone down hours earlier, and she was now working with her own body clock. The next few weeks leading up to the gallery exhibition would consist of, eat when you're hungry, and sleep when you're tired. She didn't know if she'd actually be able to sleep after finding all that shit in Andrew's apartment but she felt physically and mentally exhausted. She hoped that would be enough to knock her ass out.

She dragged her feet to the bedroom, went to the bathroom, cleaned her teeth and stripped off for bed. She turned the lights out and embraced the feel of the cold sheets against her skin as she sunk into a dreamy slumber.

The room was dark, but she could make out her dream man. He was slouched, leaning to one side, a bottle perched in his lap that looked as though it was about to crash to the floor. She raced forward and grabbed the bottle before it could fall and shatter. As she withdrew her hand with the bottle, her dream man shifted. His crossed feet fell to the floor as he tried to sit up. Chevi concluded he was drunk, "Come on big guy, let's get you to bed shall we?" She watched his head roll on his shoulders and thought to herself, 'thank god it's a dream'. He'd be too big and heavy to shift if it wasn't. She helped him to stand. She placed an arm around his waist to balance him. She lifted his arm to curl around her shoulder, to become her crutch.

He staggered, his limbs uncoordinated as they moved to where she remembered the bedroom was. He flopped onto the bed and sprawled out. She started to take his boots off then paused, 'It's a fucking dream, you moron,' she said to herself. She stood back up and using her mind, she made his clothes and boots vanish. She slapped his upper thigh saying, "Roll over big guy," he did as he was told. She pulled the sheet up over him then turned to leave. He spoke for the first time, "Stay." He lifted his hand to catch her before she left him alone again.

He looked pretty harmless in his inebriated state, and this was just a really weird dream after all, so she figured, what could it hurt?

She sat down on the side of the bed and yawned. She was tired, that's a strange concept she thought, 'I'm tired inside my own dream. What's that about?' He pulled her down next to him and encased her in his big strong arms, her head resting on his left bicep using it for a pillow. She froze when she heard him mumble, "What's your name?"

She closed her eyes and replied, "Cheval, but everyone calls me Chevi." When he started to lightly snore shortly after she answered him, she wondered if he would even remember her name when he woke. Then she realized she didn't know his. She should have asked him, but now that she thought about it she didn't want to burst that bubble by finding out his name was Frank or Eric, or something equally lame and unfitting for his stature.

She laid there listening to him breathe, his chest rose and fell against her back. She found it hypnotic. It had been so long since she'd just been held. The energy was both comforting and therapeutic and she dozed off to sleep within her dream. In this space and time, there were no dreams waiting for her, just the embrace inside the strong arms of her dream man.

MORPHEUS FELT THE ROOM'S ENERGY SHIFT. Even in his shattered state he sensed the essence of his female. She was here. She'd come to him. He felt a small amount of hope which was quickly doused with embarrassment at her seeing him this way, but in his current state which his woman thought was inebriation, he didn't have the energy to set her straight.

She helped him get to his feet, and guided him to his room, where he flopped on the bed, unable to do much else. He hadn't been this drained in, hell, he couldn't even remember. All he knew was that his female was safe from the perverted thoughts and intentions of Andrew. That he could live with. He'd manage the fallout to secure her safety.

She used her ability to manipulate his realm and made his clothes disintegrate, damn even in his weakened state he found her sexy. She lifted the sheet over his naked body, he sensed she was about to leave.

He reached out to her and in a voice not much more than a whisper he asked, "Stay."

She stood there assessing him for a minute, finally he saw the lines on her face ease with resolve, and she lay down on the bed with him. He pulled her to his chest, his face buried in her hair, he breathed deeply. An inner peace seeped through his body. With each breath, he surrendered to it, he mumbled the question he'd been searching for the answer to since the first time he saw his brown-haired beauty, "What's your name?"

He felt his female stiffen slightly, before she answered, "Cheval, but everybody calls me Chevi."

Without warning Morpheus was asleep, surrounded by nothing but empty black space, dreamless.

As the day progressed, Olivia had sent several text messages to Chevi, all of which she had not received a single response to.

The printers had sent over the invitations and Olivia's assistant had sent them all out via snail mail.

What concerned Olivia more than anything though, was that she'd missed their lunch date. They were supposed to meet with JT, a close friend who was doing the catering for the exhibit. Luckily JT didn't mind about being stood up. She ran through the numbers on the guest list and said she would put a selection of canapés together for their next meeting in a week's time at the gallery.

Olivia had given JT a couple of invitations to show remorse and smooth things over.

JT smiled and took the invites, putting them in her bag. She wasn't currently dating anyone, so for her it would be a work night, anyway. She didn't want to seem rude and figured she might know someone interested if she put her mind to it.

Morpheus woke the minute he heard incessant knocking. He opened his eyes a split second before Chevi disappeared from his embrace, and that bloody noise stopped. He wanted to hold onto her but she was gone in the blink of an eye.

He smiled. He'd finally found out what her name was. He jumped out of bed in a race to visit his brother.

He was so excited, he couldn't stop smiling. As he entered the bathroom, his reflection in the mirror was a little scary. He shrugged his shoulder, oh well something to work on. At this point he was in a hurry to visit Destiny.

Chevi stretched as she woke from her deep sleep, she rolled over to cuddle the pillow beside her. She'd slept with a body pillow for years after her chiropractor suggested it to balance her spine.

She had hurt her back falling off a horse when she was only thirteen. She never rode the stubborn mule again. In fact, she'd never ridden any horse since that day.

The neighbors had gotten too old to exercise the beast and their granddaughter had moved interstate. So her mother had dropped her in it telling them that she'd had some riding lessons with her uncle before he died. So she went over and rode the old nag. The first time in the open paddock and the bitch of a horse tried to take her under a rain shelter that was only high enough to house a horse. She'd grabbed the ledge and slid off over the horse's backside. Unable to hang on, she fell flat on her back onto a large piece of timber. It left her winded and bruised, with an aversion to horses ever since.

Her thoughts were interrupted by a pounding noise at the front door. She threw on her robe and raced to answer it.

Chevi swung the door open to be confronted by a very frantic Olivia, "Oh my god, you're alive. Thank heavens, I was about to call the police."

Chevi scratch her eyebrow to hide her amusement, "Why, what did I miss?" Confusion set in, as she spied the colorful sky splashed with a raging sunset.

"Can I come in?" Liv asked, a little worried about the way Chevi was acting.

"Um, sure," she said as she stepped back out of the way.

Liv walked toward the kitchen, "Do you have any decent coffee in this place?" She touched the coffee machine, "Guess not. It's stone cold. You missed your meeting with us today to go over the catering. We've rescheduled it for next week at the gallery. JT is going to bring a selection of things for us to choose from. We will be there anyway to start hanging some of your pieces, so it shouldn't interrupt your time." She sounded a little peeved at the inconvenience but Chevi was still a little lost.

"I thought the lunch date was set for to-morrow, I have it in my diary as Wednesday at 12:30pm, did I get the date wrong?"

Chevi nervously clenched her robe closed tighter.

"No, you're not wrong, but today is Wednesday, and it's now 4:30 in the afternoon." Liv watched Chevi's face pale. "Are you alright? I think you should sit down. You don't look so good."

Chevi landed hard in a chair at the kitchen table. "Yeah, I'm fine, just a little woozy, I thought for moment there you said it was Wednesday afternoon."

Olivia frowned, "I did,"

It took a heap of bullshit to convince Olivia that she was fine and safe to leave alone. All the while trying to convince herself of it at the same time.

She'd gone to bed on Tuesday night and slept right through till Wednesday afternoon with not a single dream. As the fog in her brain cleared, she remembered she'd had a dream about putting her dream man to bed, then nothing. Just a whole lot of black... Nada, zip, zilch, nothing.

That meant she had nothing to put on her next canvas, she thought for a second about painting a canvas entirely black and calling it something like 'The In-between.' Then giggled to herself, "Fuck me! Now I'm desperate." She continued to giggle as she went to her room to shower and dress so she could get back to her studio.

CHAPTER 9

Dream woke feeling like a new man, his energy was recharged and he was no longer sluggish and uncoordinated. He hadn't felt this great in... Forever!

Replenished and focused he showered and dressed, ready to visit his brother Destiny.

The air shifted around him suddenly and Death materialized behind him spitting out, "What the fuck are you playing at Morpheus?"

He turned and looked his brother in the eye, "My guess is, Andrew, or whatever the fuck his name was, is dead?" he said with satisfaction. He didn't care that he'd taken the balance of nature and used it to his advantage.

It wasn't like Death was as pure as the driven snow. Morpheus knew his brother had broken the rules more than a few times himself to suit his own desires. He knew this because Death had used him to aid his cause more than once. Morpheus figured 'What goes around comes around big brother.' But for Death to call him out on it, meant there had to be more to it.

"What's it to you, anyway?" He wasn't about to let Death off so easily. "You've done worse in the balance of time. Why is this Andrew so important?"

Morpheus didn't see the hit to his head coming, Death was furious. His Vanessa had vanished again. If his brother hadn't orchestrated Andrew's death, Vanessa wouldn't have seen him. She would still be working at the hospital. Where he knew exactly where to find her.

Death released all his rage at how thoughtless Morpheus's actions had been. His brother had given no thought to anyone but himself. It was selfish, and it pissed him off. He lashed out throwing punches and kicks. Not one made contact after his initial hit. He and his brother were too evenly matched, the only casualty being Dream's realm. It looked like two rival NFL teams had used his place for the Super Bowl Play-offs.

Morpheus grew tired of the battle. He sidestepped his brother's next attack and snatched up a pouch of sand.

He turned and readied for Death as he ran at him. He raised his hand palm up and blew the dream dust into his brother's face.

Death hit the floor hard, and then out cold, Morpheus stepped over him. Even though his brother probably wouldn't hear him, he said, "Clean up before you leave." He knew he'd played dirty, but he was a man on a mission and he didn't have time to wait. He'd finish this later.

Morpheus walked to the end of the hall, opened the door and entered the void that connected all the realms. He wanted. No, needed to find his female's book of destiny. He had to know what her future held. Not only for her, but for himself. He had to find out if there was a way they could be together. He'd stop at nothing to get her and keep her. The lengths he would go to were already evident. He'd never used such dirty tactics on one of his family before, but he wasn't worried about Death. He knew his brother would wake up soon enough and probably be gunning for his entrails. He laughed to himself. He would find a way to make it up to him, one day, maybe.

He clenched his fist and knocked on the door that would lead to Destiny's realm. After a while with no answer, he let himself in.

He found his brother in the library, and could hear Zandra talking to another female through the door. He felt a sudden flash of jealousy towards his oldest brother.

"Morpheus, is there something I can help you with?" Destiny inquired, startling him back from his thoughts.

"I need to find a certain book of Destiny. Can I have access to your library?" he replied, not that he was going to take no for an answer, but he thought it was polite to at least ask.

Destiny raised his hand in the general direction of the shelves saying, "Knock yourself out. I'd stay and help but I promised Zandra I'd take care of something for her."

Morpheus's jealous streak deepened at hearing his brother's words. He reminded himself again he was a man on his own mission and his goal was to have and keep his own female. Destiny could go and fuck himself as he began his search through the journals.

Morpheus gave up looking for Cheval's book. It wasn't there. He grew more and more frenzied in his search until finally he resolved that maybe she'd lied to him about her name, maybe it was because he only had her first name. Regardless, his quest had ended with the realization that things were not going play out the way he planned. Therefore, he would have to come up with another way.

At least until he worked out how to get into her head when she was awake, there had to be some way for him to harness her daydreams.

Chevi had about a half an hour before her appointment with Harley. She was going over to his shop to check on the front window design and add to her collection of tattoos while she was there. She always remembered a story her Nana had told her as a little girl, about mayflies and how they only live for one day. The motto of the story was that no matter how long you have, you have to live life to the fullest. So she had sketched up two mayfly's dancing together. She planned to have them done on her ribs. She had a bag of sweets to suck on to keep her energy up. She was actually looking forward to it, now that it was going to happen.

She put everything into her bag, snatched up her car keys and locked the door behind her. She only felt a smidgen of guilt for not using the time to paint. She promised herself she would dedicate the next three days solely to the preparation of the exhibition.

Chevi climbed into her red mini, buckled her seatbelt and started the engine.

She had fallen in love with the lipstick-red color the instant she'd seen it on the showroom floor. The salesman tried to tell her that it was a four to six week wait on an off the line new one. She remembered the horrified look on his face when she told him, "I have cash to spend and if I don't leave here in the next hour with the signed paperwork for that," she pointed at the lipstick red one. "I'll be going down the road to buy a beautiful VW Gulf," He had no idea she was lying. He'd gone to speak with the manager. When he returned he told her, "The manager has instructed me to let you have it and to give you two thousand cash back because you're paying cash. If you'd like to follow me, we can get the paperwork done."

She may not be rolling in dough, but she lived comfortably. She had her apartment and her car, with a little spending left over. She smiled, she loved the barter system. She was getting a free tattoo plus some change under the table for doing the design at Harley's. She turned into the car park and parked. As this was the first chance to see the window design finished, she grabbed her bag and raced for the front of the shop. She couldn't help herself as she rifled in the side pocket of her bag for her phone to take pictures. She could add it to her portfolio. She was about to overstep the gutter into the oncoming traffic when Harley took her by the arm, "Hey, careful there, doll," he said as she glanced over her shoulder just in time to see a car swerve to miss her.

"Damn, I need to pay more attention to my surroundings." Laughing, she added, "I was so distracted I didn't even see you come out."

"I didn't. I came from across the road, they have the most amazing pancakes, and the coffees' not bad either." He smiled. "Are you ready for this? I've got everything set up and ready to go."

She gave a nod, "Yep, let's do this. Hang on a sec, I have to ask, are you happy with how the front window turned out?"

Harley slapped her on the back and grinned with satisfaction, "It's fucking awesome, absolutely perfect. Now let's get this show on the road?"

As the first touch of the tattoo needles

on her naked ribs started, Harley said, "Welcome back." The sensation was like a hot pen tip moving over her skin. She smiled in the mirror in front of her, "Thanks, now if you don't mind I'd like to meditate. Don't stop, you know I'm not passed out." It was a long-standing joke from the first time she'd let Harley tattoo her. She'd been tired from pulling an all-nighter and had slept through most of it. He'd called her a freak, but as he finished up, she'd started feel a little tender. A big burly biker had walked in at the same time to start his tattoo with Harley's colleague, Dan. It still cracked her up when she thought about it, as soon as the needle brushed his skin, he turned as white as a sheet and passed out. He came round about twenty minutes later to ask was it done. Regardless to say, he was probably the only biker in the gang that didn't have tattoos. Maybe that was something she could add to her list of paintings for the exhibit. People often dreamed about having a tattoo, but some after getting one saw them as a nightmare.

Two and a half hours later, Harley

started to push some white into the finishing touches, "Okay, now I'm feeling it," she admitted.

Harley laughed, "Almost done, doll. I wish everyone could stay as still as you do. Most of the time they are wriggling all over the place." He put the gun down, sprayed her skin and wiped it clean of blood and excess ink. He wiped it over with balm, slapped her ass and told her to have a look before he covered it in clear film and taped down the edges. It was perfect, just what she'd asked for. She gave Harley a kiss on the cheek and left after collecting the difference for the front window design.

CHAPTER 10

By the time Chevi arrived home it was going on for 9:30pm. She was Harley's last appointment for the day. She had no idea what she felt like having for dinner but she knew the bag of sweets she'd consumed before and after getting her tattoo done, was not part of the five food groups. She didn't feel much like cooking so she settled for soup in a cup and some toast.

She sat at the table with her sketch pad while she ate. Intent on playing with an idea she'd had for her next piece.

She quickly finished the last couple of mouthfuls of her cold soup, rinsed her dishes and was eager to get started. She wouldn't be satisfied until she had at least a total of ten pieces.

She worked diligently to complete the open-mouthed nightmare on the easel, before moving on to the next one. As she moved the painting to a drying easel, and replaced it with a large fresh, stark white, naked canvas, she suddenly felt a flutter of panic and apprehension. Self-doubt took root, she started to question whether she was going to get things done on time. She began to think maybe she should cancel or postpone the show. Either way, her hands possessed that sensation, the tingle that told her they had to work, they were itching to create.

Chevi took a few calming breaths to ward off her fears and picked up her tools of the trade.

DREAM HAD RETURNED TO HIS REALM, feeling quite disheartened. He sank into his chair, leaned forward and placed his head in both hands. He was at a loss for a solution to his problem, and he was sick and tired of sporting a hard-on for his female. It was becoming unbearably painful.

At least if nothing else, Death was gone, along with the mess from their rumble earlier. He reminisced about the fights he and his brothers had when they were young. Once they realized they couldn't kill each other, some of their battles had become brutal, until they got bored and grew out of it. He still couldn't grasp how his mother had managed to tolerate them all.

He scented her floral fragrance before the air shimmered. He sighed and lifted his head. 'Just fucking great!' he thought to himself, as his eyes met those of his almighty absent mother.

He couldn't resist poking her ego with an electric cattle prod. "Hello Cosmo, I'm Morpheus. Nice to make your acquaintance. What brings you here?" he jibbed.

Cosmo raised her hand and with the flick of her wrist, Morpheus was against the wall, pinned unable to move. "Silence!" She commanded. "I will not tolerate such insubordination. How dare you! When I've come to aid you in your dilemma, perhaps I shouldn't have bothered."

"What do you know about my circumstances? You haven't been to see me since, shit I can't even remember the last time I saw you." he snarled back at his mother.

She looked away from her son, too ashamed to admit she cried for him behind closed doors. She knew he'd been slowly losing his mind. She herself had been in the same head space a very long time ago. Cosmo had watched her beautiful baby boy grow up to be a dream weaver. He was the only one of her children with the ability. She had passed on to him what he surely saw as a curse, and it was. But it was also a gift and it would lead him to his beloved. She'd been watching him closely from her realm and suspected that he'd met his equal. A very rare human with the power to dream walk. Morpheus would continue to slip further into madness until he claimed his female. Cosmo had known of her son's human dreamwalker from the moment of her birth and had been waiting for her to be recognized.

Even though Cosmo sympathized with her son's insomnia, she couldn't go back to being the Dreamweaver she was prior to Morpheus's twenty-first cycle. It had been a long battle for her to regain her own sanity, and even now, it was questionable.

Cosmo approached her son, 'Morpheus, The Lord of Dreams.' She raised a shaky hand to his cheek, as a tear trailed down her saddened face, "You may feel like I've abandoned you my precious one, but I love you dearly and if I could free you from your duties, I would. You are my strength and my weakness. I wouldn't have chosen this life for you if I didn't think you were the only one capable of surviving this realm." She placed her free hand on Dream's other cheek, pulled his head down to kiss his forehead. As she pulled back, she whispered, "I love you."

Her unspent tears threatening to overflow tore at Morpheus's fractured mind, "Save me mother, please, before it's too late." he begged. "If you love me as you say you do, then save me."

He blinked away the tingle of his own

tears trying to form, his mother faded and disappeared. He used the wall to help keep him vertical, sucking air deeply into his lungs. Once his composure was back, he pushed off the wall. He immediately made a beeline to his desk drawer where he could attack the bottle of scotch. With the bottle in his hand, he started to lift it to his lips when he spied a thick leather bound volume on the centre of his desk. He stood the bottle down beside it and ran his fingertips over the well-worn ancient script. He spoke the word as his brain registered what his mother had given him, a spark of hope, "Dreamwalker."

CHAPTER 11

Chevi kept herself occupied into the early hours of the morning. She'd lost all concept of time until the perspiration under the plastic covering her latest tattoo began to sting like a bitch. Her muscles were starting to twitch and spasm. Reluctantly, she yawned and prepared to call it a night. She placed her brushes in solvent, then turned and switched off the light.

Once in her bathroom, she lifted her shirt over her head, removed the protective layer from her tat, then took off the rest of her clothes and stepped into the shower, "Fuck me! Son of a bitch! Mofo...!" She cursed loudly, as the hot water hit the inked artwork. She'd forgotten how much that shit hurt. It reminded her of the worst case of sunburn, the nerves stung, and her flesh felt like it was on fire. Working up a lather, she washed the old cream and excess ink off, then hurried through the rest of her shower. Towel dried and with fresh cream applied, she climbed into her unmade bed and fell asleep within minutes.

Through the darkness emerged the image of her dream lover. He was sitting at his desk, his attention focused on a book. His fingers at the top of the page in preparation of turning it to the next one, she froze, as his head lifted and his gaze honed in on her.

Morpheus's cock hardened instantly, he wanted her so badly his entire body ached. If only half of what he'd been reading were true, then he was more determined than ever to bind her to him. Even if it was only in their dreams. He would find a way to keep her here. Granted, it would be tricky, but he'd figure it out... Somehow.

Chevi could feel his eyes on her like a physical touch, the way she wanted his hands to caress her curves and hollows. Her pussy tightened with the need to feel him skin to skin, her blood pulsed through her so hard she could hear it.

He slowly stood and tentatively started to stalk closer, testing the seams of her dreamscape. If he moved too quickly, she might spook. He wanted her to believe she was in control, even if it wasn't entirely true.

He circled her like she was the lamb and he was the lion. He heard his woman's breath hitch, curious to find out if it was fear or maybe... something else. The energy in the room surrounding them sizzled like the impending strike of a lightning bolt.

Close enough to touch, yet the distance between them was still too far. He took a step closer and swept her long brown hair over her shoulders. His fingers brushed her skin. Goosebumps rose to cover her arms. She shivered in anticipation. He placed a kiss at the base of her neck and her nipples peeked so hard it bordered on painful.

She leaned into the distance, separating their bodies, trusting he would be there.

Chevi's back met her dream lover's chest, his desire for her evident in the hollow just above the curve of her backside.

She closed her eyes and held her breath as she felt her face flush, her thoughts of what she wanted to do to him and have done to her were erotic and sinful.

The air around them shifted. Surprised, she opened her eyes. They were no longer in the centre of the room. With a gasp, she tried to retreat. He now stood directly in front of her, his desk had been but a fleeting heated scene behind her closed eyes.

Morpheus's heart raced as the air surrounding them warped, 'Damn it!' he thought. He held back his curse once he was aware she hadn't vanished. His female had manipulated her dream, he stepped closer boxing her in. Her rear met the edge of his desk. He smirked, 'This is workable.' he thought to himself.

One hand slid into her hair, the other around to cup her ass, as his lips took possession of hers, and he pulled her firmly against his need. This time he wasn't taking any chances, he was taking prisoners. He would leave her branded by his desire.

He would be on her mind regardless of sleep.

His hand left her body long enough to swipe his desk clean, and everything crashed to the floor. He eased her back to rest against its hard surface. Next time, he would concern himself about airs and graces, but this time, his need was greater than niceties. Crazed, he disintegrated her clothing.

He covered her body with his and possessed her lips. Tongues testing and tasting, he nipped her bottom lip, until neither could breathe. Finally he broke the bond and kissed down her neck. He circled her erect nipple, flicking over it several times before suckling it between his kiss-swollen lips.

Chevi moaned in ecstasy, her body tingled with need, her pussy throbbed. Unable to sustain the torture any longer, she lifted her hand placed it on the top of his head and applied pressure.

Morpheus growled as his attention was

directed lower, his female taking command of her needs. His cock felt strangled by his own clothes, but he knew in his current state he couldn't chance removing them. He wanted to take care of his woman first, she would always mean that much to him.

Chevi lifted her legs, but without anything to put them on she knew it would be too difficult to stay that way for long.

Morpheus noticed the movement and dragged his chair closer to the desk. One at a time, he lifted her legs. As he placed kisses to the inside of each, he sat them on the arms.

Morpheus's eyes became transfixed on the most exquisite sight he had ever seen. His stunningly beautiful brown-haired beauty splayed for his admiration.

Determined to worship her, he lowered his head and kissed her shaved mons.

Chevi rolled her hips, lifting to give encouragement, as she gently pinched her nipples between her fingers. Her back arched when she felt his tongue part her swollen lips and slide down over her inflamed bud. She cried out in pleasure, liquid heat gushed from her pussy to meet the stimulation of his tongue as he penetrated her entrance.

With her body on fire and needing more, she lowered her hand to finish the job. She wasn't sure how much more of this she could stand.

Morpheus intercepted the approach of her hand. He lifted his head and shook it from side to side, making a tsk tsk, noise with his juicy lips and tongue. Chevi whimpered, she attempted to regain control, but he was much stronger than her and somehow managed to trap both her hands in just one of his. With a firm grip of the situation, he anchored their conjoined hands on her belly.

She was spellbound by the hypnotic gleam in his eyes, as he inserted one finger then another, her eyes rolled back inside her head. He lowered his lips to French kiss her over-sensitive jewel, as he curled his finger tips to blanch her G-spot.

She screamed as her orgasm ruptured, ripping through her, it struck like lightning. So intense it took her breath away, and her vision wavered. "Arrrrgh!" Chevi collapsed in a gooey mess, her pussy still pulsing around his finger, "Who are you?" she gasped.

Morpheus stood, blinked his clothes away, and quickly replied, "Sandy," as he gripped his throbbing cock at her entrance and thrust soul deep in one forceful stroke. He lifted her legs over his forearms, his palms flat on the table beside her hips. He waited, not game to move. The tightness of her inner muscles threatened his sanity, and he didn't want to hurt her with his savage need.

Chevi's hands circled his thick wrists, "Moooove..." She begged, "Please, Sandy move." His cock was so deep the head rested against her cervix. She could feel his pulse.

He slowly withdrew past the convulsing muscles, still an inch inside, before he immersed his hardness again. His slow orchestration was torture; she dug her fingernails into his flesh. He sucked air through his teeth, his jaw locked in concentration. He growled, "Now! Cum for me now, I wanna feel you come apart around my cock." He jack-hammered into her, unrestrained. He held nothing back as he buried himself deep. His hot seed surged up his length, and exploded, filling his woman's vault.

Chevi matched him stroke for powerful stroke, the dirty talk, intoxicating. She imploded, her inner walls convulsed tighter with increasing pressure, as her orgasm erupted.

The experience was so foreign, she almost lost consciousness. Well fucked, she collapsed. She didn't even have the energy to speak, but one word came to mind, 'Ruined.' He'd ruined her for any other man.

Nobody would ever be able to match her imaginary lover. A tear rolled from the corner of her eye, trailing down into her hair.

Morpheus could barely stand. He felt like his soul had been sucked out of his body. He would do that again in a heartbeat forever, he just needed to sit down for a minute to recover. He collected his female into his arms and carried her to his bed, his length still encased by his mate's body.

Their bodies separated as he laid them down, he cuddled her close, "Stay with me while I sleep?" he asked; the lost look in his eyes nearly broke her heart. She could find it way too easy to fall in love with him, she knew she shouldn't but when he looked at her like that, she couldn't deny him. She nodded.

He sighed with relief, then kissed her. Kissing him back, an amazing sense of peace and contentment washed over her. It was on the tip of her tongue to say words that seemed ridiculous, she'd only just met him and this was after all, a fucking dream.

She snuggled closer, "I love you," she said, you could say and do anything you wanted in a dream. She heard his heartbeat pick up. She smiled, as her eyes fluttered closed.

Morpheus had startled at the words his female had spoken. When he had moved past the initial shock of the moment, and was about to say something, he saw she'd fallen asleep in his arms. Exactly right where she belonged. He closed his eyes to savor the tranquility of the moment, interwoven with an inner calm which lulled him to sleep.

CHAPTER 12

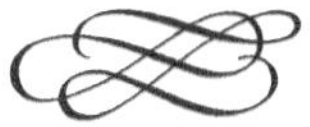

Chevi opened her eyes to find a sculptured chest, rising and falling under her hand, as it came into focus. Her artistic streak surfaced. She rose to sit cross legged next to her Dream man.

She wished she had her sketchpad and pencil, she glanced around, next to the bed on the night-stand she found what she craved.

Slowly she leaned over and claimed it. She thought it was weird but still pretty cool. She opened the cover to reveal the first page, and began to draw, tilting her pencil this way and that, to alter the dimensions of her creation with a smudge here and a shade there. She was about half way through her sketch when she raised her eyes to examine his perfect physique to find him watching her.

Heat flushed her cheeks, she'd been sprung. Worse, she was butt naked and sitting cross legged.

"What are you doing?" he asked, with a puzzled look across his face.

Embarrassment caused the words to stick in her throat. She coughed, "Um, I'm sketching," She averted her eyes, back to her work, "You."

"Can I see?" He wanted to learn everything about her, he wanted to know what made her happy, what made her sad. What sort of food she liked, what she didn't. What she did in the human realm, but right now all he could think about was how gorgeous she looked sitting on his bed.

"It's not finished yet," she told him as she turned the page to face him.

He smiled as he examined the detail she had captured. He couldn't help but have pride in such a talented female, his female.

"You're very good, I'm impressed," he said, handing the piece back to her.

"Thanks, I need to be, it's how I make my living," she replied.

Her stomach growled loudly, letting her know it had been a while since she'd eaten. She looked around the room, "Do you have a bathroom I can use?"

He laughed, "Yeah it's through that door." He pointed her in the right direction.

She walked into the huge room, used the toilet, then called out to him, "Do you mind if I have a shower?"

"Knock yourself out, there's towels under the basin, I'll find you a shirt to wear." He liked the idea of seeing her in one his shirts. He materialized one in his hand, then tapped on the bathroom door. There was no answer, but all of a sudden he was standing inside the shower. He instantly knew it wasn't him that had made that happen. She smiled and asked, "What took you so long?"

"I was getting you something to wear," he said, looking at the saturated shirt in his hand. She followed the direction of his stare, she laughed and made it vanish. It then reappeared with a thwack as it hit the floor of the tub next to the shower.

"Damn! This shit is too cool," she exclaimed as she enjoyed her ability to manipulate her surroundings.

Unable to resist touching each other, they washed one another. They stoked the fires building between them, as they memorized every curve and mound, plain and muscle.

He leaned down to nuzzle her ear and kiss her neck. He licked the rivulets coursing their way down her body, he went down on one knee, ran his tongue around her navel, then laughed, as Chevi's stomach responded with a growl. "I guess I should feed you?" He stood and turned the water off. They stepped out onto the bath mat and made quick work of drying themselves. Wrapped in towels, Morpheus took her by the hand, raised it to his lips and kissed it. "Come on, let see what's to eat?" He suggested, leading her to the kitchen.

He opened the fridge to find his sister, sweet heartedness, had filled the shelves again. He paused with his hand on the door,

"What do you feel like? Sweet or savory?" He stood in the way so she couldn't see the contents.

"Pancakes with caramelized banana, maple syrup and ice cream," she decided.

"Wow, sounds delicious, but I have no idea what it is or how to make it." He told himself he'd have to learn.

He turned to rattle off a list of what he had to see a plate on the bench, Chevi had moved to the drawer to find cutlery, "Come and try some, tell me what you think?" She coaxed.

She loaded the fork with a little of everything and raised it to his mouth. His stomach rumbled at the aroma. He opened his mouth for his female, thinking she liked him enough to feed him. He closed his lips around the fork, as the food hit his taste buds he moaned, he had a food orgasm exploding on his tongue. He moaned again before swallowing and licking his lips clean. "That's fucking delicious!" She had heaven on a plate. He wondered if maybe she'd be happy to share.

He lifted the plate, with its decadent flavor, smiled and said, "Okay, I know what I'm having. What about you?"

She laughed and made his absconded food disappear. "Hey, now that wasn't very nice," he pouted.

He hadn't had enough of the dish to be able to recreate it for himself. She passed him a fork from the drawer, she liked the way he watched her as she moved. His entire attention locked on her, it made her less self-conscious of the fact she couldn't take her eyes off of him either.

"There's enough for both of us." She grinned at the two plates she'd just put on the bench, the aroma of freshly percolated coffee filled the room. "I think that's everything we need."

She went to move around him to get to her breakfast, his hand shot out catching her on the way past, "I could get used to this," he said, as he kissed her tenderly. The next time they were together he'd be more gentle, loving. He'd only spent a short amount of time with his female but his heart had been invested from the first time he'd caught sight of her.

Chevi's arms circled his neck, she kissed him back, tasting and teasing. When she broke the kiss she whispered, "Me too," with a sadness she understood to mean she had no idea how long this dream would last.

They sat at the kitchen bench beside each other, but to Chevi, it felt like they were on opposite sides of the Grand Canyon. They ate silently neither one able to put their thoughts into words.

After breakfast, Chevi stood. She faced him, placing her hand on his cheek, and she leaned down and brushed her lips against his. "I really should be going. I have a lot of work to do." Her words left a bitter-sweet taste in her mouth.

"I'd really like it if you'd stay, just a little longer?" He couldn't help it, he had to ask.

She detected the loneliness in his voice, and could feel her own longing tug at her heart, "Alright, but can I set up a place so I can make some memories? And it's on one condition, you have to sit for me."

"I think I understand what you're looking for, but I have a better idea first."

Morpheus stood, collected her hand and led her to his library.

He took out a pouch of sand from his desk drawer, then sat in his chair and pulled her into his lap. He kissed her briefly, then asked her to close her eyes. He scattered the sand over the globe and closed the bag. He tossed the bag back on his desk, wrapped his arms around his woman and closed his eyes.

He checked the connection between them and confirmed he could hear and see her and she him. It felt more intimate than any kiss. Sharing each other's thoughts.

He searched for a dreamer...

Chevi followed his instructions filled with nervous excitement. It was like playing a game for the first time, with no idea what to expect.

With her eyes closed, she could hear a shuffle of movement, then she felt his arms encase her.

The room was quiet, except for their breathing. She focused on his breaths so she could match them. Relaxing into his body, behind her eyes was dark. She jumped a little when she heard his voice inside her head, yet he hadn't spoken aloud. He asked, "I find you intriguing and beautiful. I would like to take you on a date. This is the only way I know how. Keep your eyes closed and watch through my eyes. I want to show you the beauty of my world."

She didn't answer. She couldn't think of anything to say, anyway.

"Don't say anything. We have no need for words where we're going." She laid her head on his shoulder and gave him control.

Out of the shadows, she saw a glimpse of light. The image became clearer, it was a little girl sitting in a wheelchair, she was crying. From the mist-encased woods surrounding her, came a beautiful horse with a flowing mane. It walked up to the girl, then bowed its head to nuzzle her hand. It stomped its hoof to say 'come on, come on.' The little girls face suddenly lit up, her smile went all the way to her eyes. The horse moved, then bowed down for her to climb onto its back. She began to giggle and laugh as the horse stood up. Walking at first, before picking up the pace to a trot, then a canter, it was only a short ride tonight, but she was happy to just be riding. The horse returned her to where the wheelchair was stationed, lowered itself for her to climb off and waited for the ritual kiss on the nose. As the little girl sighed and returned to her wheelchair, the image faded.

Chevi was about to ask questions when another light came to life. This time it was an old man, he was sick in a hospital bed. The room was empty, but he was talking to someone. "I'll be home soon my love, not long now." The image then became that of a much younger man, in his early twenties. He was dressed in a tuxedo, standing in a room that resembled the ones seen in chapels. Another man, around the same age, walked in. He didn't appear happy to be there, but was dressed in a tuxedo as well. He fidgeted with something in his pocket, then said, "It's not too late to back out, are you sure you really want to do this?"

The man she guessed to be a groom, turned and sneered, "You're supposed to be my brother, and that means standing by the decisions and choices I make. If you can't be happy for me, then you need to leave. I love my Daphne, and nothing you can say or do will ever change that. Are we done here? My bride is waiting."

The next scene was the look of love in Daphne's eyes as she said, "I do," and the minister pronounced them husband and wife.

From there, it became the image of the man now in his late twenties, pacing back and forth as he waited for the cry of his first-born child. The nurse walking towards him saying, "It's a beautiful healthy baby girl."

The picture shimmered again, and he was back in the church, a much older man. His wife would have loved to see their Sonia get married, to have danced at her wedding. He danced with Sonia as the father of the bride.

She then saw a room full of noisy grand-kids racing and tearing around an enor-mous Christmas tree, all screaming to open their presents.

He missed his Daphne every day. Fi-nally he was back in the hospital room. He held an old woman in his arms and lulled her to sleep, playing with her hair. The image faded away the same as the little girl's had.

Finally Chevi had a moment to ask a question, "So are these memories or dreams, as in hopes and dreams, things people wish were true?"

Morpheus replied, "All and everything. Are you ready to go?"

"Go? Go where? I thought we were already there." She was a little confused now, not sure what he planned next.

Out of the darkness, a woman dressed in an exquisite evening gown. It was such a deep blood red it almost looked black. Her chocolate hair was up in a fantasy up-style. She wore gems set in gold around her neck and from her ears. Chevi inhaled sharply, "Oh my god, is that me? I'm beautiful." Her artist's eyes engraving the image into her subconscious.

Morpheus whispered softly through her mind, "Stunning. Shhh, just watch."

Obediently she quietened, eager to see what was going on. The light brightened slightly. The dress's fabric draped and scooped in all the right places. From behind the elegant version of herself, Chevi could see what looked a lot like the gallery she was booked to hold her exhibit in. The lighting dim and seductive, the paintings under a soft hue to accentuate the layers trapped on what was once a flat white canvas.

Chevi walked around, inspecting all the artwork to ensure everything was perfect. Her heels clicking on the marble floor, she lifted her gown and turned, when she was tapped on the shoulder by a waiter offering flutes of wine.

With the nod of her head, she thanked him. She saw a shadow of movement from the corner. Then the dream faded away.

"My gift to you was showing you how your artistic ability astounds me. You astound me. You can open your eyes now." He whispered against her ear. He kissed down her neck and along her jaw. His lips took possession of hers as she tilted her head back.

It was a combustion of energy between the two, was it meant to mean welcome home? Stay? Or will I ever see you again, goodbye?

The things he'd shown her were as priceless as the gems she'd worn with the red gown. She didn't want to leave. She wanted to stay forever. In his world, she felt at home... But she had to go.

CHAPTER 14

Chevi woke with her head on a tear-soaked pillow. Olivia was standing over the bed, tapping her shoulder and calling her name.

When Olivia saw her open her eyes, she gasped, "Good Lord, I was beginning to think you were dead. I've been trying to reach you for days."

Chevi jumped up and looked around the room. Nothing seemed out of place.

She snatched up her mobile phone from the night stand and remembered she'd switched it off so she wouldn't be woken by it. As she turned it back on, she noticed she was wearing different clothes to the ones she'd worn to bed, she was now dressed in a man's oversized T-shirt. "Shit!" She said, as her phone started beeping with text messages and missed calls.

"I'm sorry Olivia. I'm not sure what happened. Can you excuse me a minute? I need to use the bathroom." She made her way to the toilet, used it, and washed her hands. She looked at her reflection in the mirror over the basin, and washed her face to freshen up too, then joined Olivia, who was now downstairs in the studio.

"Well at least you've been busy," she said as she looked at all the completed work. "So how many more pieces are you hoping to put into the show?" she asked, obviously thinking that Chevi had been dodging her calls the entire time.

"How long before we can move some of these to the gallery? It would free up some extra space for you to work. I have my SUV out the front. I could lower the back seats and load them in now. I'm on my way to meet JT at the gallery, anyway. She wants to see the layout in preparation for the catering."

"Okay, just give me a minute to take photos of them," she said opening the camera application on her phone, and snapping off several shots. "Okay, that's the last of them, I'll help you load them into your car, then grab a quick shower and meet you at the gallery. It'll give me a chance to see how and where I want them hung."

"Sounds like a good plan to me," said Olivia, as she lifted one of the smaller pieces.

Once the last piece was loaded, she waved Olivia off, and raced upstairs to get showered and changed.

DREAM WALKED THROUGH HIS REALM LIKE A zombie, a damn lonely one. He needed someone to talk to. He didn't want to be alone in his misery. He showered and dressed, thinking maybe his brother Destiny could help him.

ZANDRA HAD LEFT IVA AT HOME SO SHE could have some girl time with JT. They went shopping and spent the morning doing the rounds in all the shops at the mall.

They stopped to have coffee in a quaint little café. JT asked how things were for her now that she was a full-time stay at home mum. Zandra replied, "It's great, a little hard to have time to myself some days. I don't remember the last time I had a day where I had my hair done, a mani-pedi, or a massage. Overall though, life is good." She smiled at the thought of Destiny at home with Iva, doing finger painting and playing tea parties. "Des has been hinting at us to have another baby, but I'm not sure if I'm ready yet. I've gained a few pounds since having Iva and Des's sister Faith keeps bringing us these delicious eats she insists on making. I think she's lonely," Zandra said, trying to change the subject.

"I like sweets. Maybe she would be interested in helping out with my catering sometime," JT offered. "You'll have to introduce us. I could always use an extra set of hands, especially if she can cook."

"I might just do that, maybe see if she'd be interested in planning a menu for a family dinner party." Zandra liked the idea.

"Speaking of parties, are you interested in an art exhibition? It's called 'Dreams and Nightmares,' by an artist Olivia knows, Cheval, something?" JT was digging through some paperwork inside her PDA folder. Pulling one of the invitations out, she glanced at it and added, "Cheval Noland, that's it. I know it's short notice but you might be able to line up a sitter for Iva. After all, how long has it been since you and Des had a night out?"

Zandra took the invitation and looked it over. It sounded intriguing. "Put us down as a yes." She went to pass the second one back and JT waved her hand at her saying, "No keep it, I don't know anyone else I'd give it to, and it'll only clutter up my paperwork."

"Well, I hate to bring the fun to an end, but work beckons. I have to meet Olivia at the gallery, to find out where I can set things up for the catering. You're sure you don't mind tagging along before I take you home?" JT had scheduled the appointment earlier in the week and didn't want to miss the opportunity to confirm the details with the gallery owner and artist.

Zandra replied, "Not at all, seeing as I dragged you away from work to spend the morning with me." She finished the last mouthful of coffee, collected up her shopping bags and said, "Lead me to your chariot."

"You wouldn't be taking the piss out of my mighty steed, now would you?" JT laughed.

CHEVI RACED INTO THE BACK DOOR OF THE gallery just as it started to rain, her sneakers squeaking on the timber floors.

"Careful!" Olivia called out, "We can't afford any broken bones this close to opening night," racing to the rear door with a towel for the floor. "I hope this rain doesn't set in, I only managed to get one painting inside before it started, so I'll have to wait it out before the rest can be brought in." She sighed with her hand on her hip as if the weather was out to ruin her life.

"Can I get you to send me a copy of the pictures you took before we loaded them? That way I can make a note to indicate where we'll hang them, and it won't hold you up any longer than necessary."

"Sure, I'm ready to start when you are," she said as she walked down the hall into the main area of the gallery.

"Oh, you seem to have visitors," Chevi pointed at two women standing at the locked entry.

Olivia asked, "Could you let them in while get some more towels?" She rushed off in the opposite direction.

Chevi walked to the door, unlocked it and swung it open. "Hi. Olivia is just getting you some towels, she won't be a minute." She would guess the women to be around her age maybe a year or two older.

Olivia re-entered the room with an arm full of towels. "JT, this Chevi Noland, she's the artist we'll be honoring on the night."

Zandra felt a little out of place. She noticed somewhat of an awkward moment of silence as she watched JT and Chevi shake hands. JT introduced Zandra and mentioned that Zandra would be attending the opening night on the guest list. They then got down to business, going through the list of canapés and wines, and the choice of champagne for the toast.

Zandra's attention was transfixed on the painting leant up against the wall.

JT nudged her, "Are you alright?" she whispered. "You look a little spaced out."

Zandra smiled, "Yes, yes I'm fine, just a little preoccupied." She gestured towards the art piece, and inquired, "Chevi, I hope you don't mind me asking, but where do you draw you inspiration from."

Chevi blushed, "My dreams," she answered.

Morpheus knocked on the door before entering Destiny's realm. He opened it and called out, "Anybody home?"

Destiny stuck his head out of the kitchen and waved him in, "I'm down here," before going back to the table. He placed a cup of juice next to Iva, then looked up at his brother as he entered.

"You laugh and you can leave the same way you came in," he said smiling at his brother.

Morpheus held up both hands in surrender. He pulled out a chair and sat across from his brother, "I hope you don't mind me busting in on your father daughter time?"

His brother looked to be of a lucid mind, but he noted a sound of longing. He told him, "No, but the penalty is you have to partake in the activities." He passed Dream a brush and paper.

They didn't talk at first. Destiny didn't know what brought his brother here today, and he wasn't going to dig. He figured if he had something to say he would... eventually.

Morpheus sat entranced by the white piece of paper. After several minutes, he dipped the brush, as he lifted it to the paper, he said, "Are you and Zandra happy?"

Destiny studied him before he answered, "I'd say yes, we still have our disagreements, but overall we are. Why, what's this about? I know you didn't come here to do kiddy painting." He continued to watch his brother, who didn't seem to want eye contact.

Morpheus thought about it long and hard then with a sigh he told Destiny most of what had been happening. As he finished explaining the things he was comfortable to mention, Zandra walked into the room.

Zandra felt guilty for interrupting the conversation, "Sorry, didn't mean to intrude, just wanted to let you know I was home." She gave her daughter a once over, "You are going to magically clean all this up when you're done. Right?" She kissed the top of Iva's head, then stepped sideways to brush her lips over her husband's face. "Did you miss me?" she smiled.

"Yes, I always do." He answered wrapping his arms around her waist pulling her close.

The day played on her mind for a second before her attention returned to their guest.

"I should be going," Dream mumbled feeling like the intruder.

"Wait Sandy, I know we don't know each

other all that well, but..." She tried to find a way to get to the point and tactful wasn't in the equation. "Do you love her?"

Both men said, "What?" Looking at her like she had three heads and was dressed in a gorilla suit. Yeah, she probably could have worded that a little better.

"Okay, sit, stay." She pointed at Morpheus. She raced to where she'd thrown her bags inside the front door.

"Is she always this intense?" Dream tried not to offend his brother by picking on Zandra.

"If you mean intense as in bossy, then yes, she has her moments." He laughed.

Zandra came back into the room waving the invitations. She handed one to each of them. "I had the privilege of meeting said artist, Chevi Noland today at the gallery her exhibition is being held at. JT is doing the catering for it." She looked at her husband. "There was only one painting inside when we arrived." She looked at Morpheus "Sandy, it was of you."

CHAPTER 15

Chevi was pretty happy with how the plans were coming together for opening night. Drawing from the images from her dream, she explained that she wanted sheer fabric sheets suspended from the ceiling to hang like curtains. She felt it would lend an intimacy between the viewer and the art. Because all the walls inside the gallery were stark white, she wanted low lighting to create a night ambiance to the room, and soft light to be focused on the individual compositions.

She drove home through the drizzle, parked her car, and went inside. Her clothes were still damp from getting caught in the rain earlier. She kicked off her shoes at the front door and headed straight to the bathroom. She peeled off her garments and turned on the heater, then ran a hot bath. She was chilled to the bone. She took the bottle of soft musk bath essence from the cupboard under the sink, added it to the water, and watched as the bubbles foamed. When the tub was three-quarters full, she turned the water off, rolled up a towel and stepped in, pausing just long enough for her ass to stop burning as it touched the water's steaming surface. She positioned the rolled towel behind her head as she relaxed back. Her legs spread and slightly bent, she wished the damn thing was bigger, like the one from her dream.

She closed her eyes letting the heat seep into her bones, moaning softly with contentment. Her mind became blank, releasing all thoughts from the day. She wasn't going to think about how she'd lost time or days. She needed to find something to paint from inside herself.

～

ONE MINUTE, MORPHEUS WAS IN HIS REALM sitting at his desk reading more of the book his mother had given him regarding his female. The next minute, he was naked in a hot tub with Chevi. He blinked twice, watching her moan as she laid there with her eyes closed. Well at least she wasn't fantasizing about another man, he could live with that.

He lifted her foot, and kissed her instep, her eyes flashed open, and she sunk down under the water with a squeaked "Fu...!" She resurfaced, pushing her wet hair out of her face and suds from her eyes and chin. He smiled at how adorable she looked.

"What the fuck?" She looked around. This wasn't her place. She'd done it again. 'Would this shit never end?' she thought. Not that she was complaining about the co-habitant of the dream being in the tub with her.

Obviously, her under-sexed brain had decided she needed some lovin'.

She blinked and found herself straddling her man's lap, "Hi," she smiled.

Goosebumps appeared over Morpheus's

exposed skin. The sultry sound of her voice and her chest pressed against his made him shiver in anticipation. His cock stiffened instantly as she licked up the side of his neck. She sucked his earlobe between her lips. This time she was in the position of power, and he found it interestingly hot. He loved how uninhibited she was with him.

She sat on his lap, trapping his hardness between them. He encased her in his strong arms, adding to her body's pressure against him.

She leant away from him, arching her back over his forearms, exposing her luscious breasts.

His eyes followed down the curve of her neck to the tip of her nipple, he licked his lips wanting to taste her cherries. His tongue trailed from the underside of her mound up to conquer the peak.

He brushed it with his lips, his tongue skirted the areola. As her hands lifted from his shoulders to dive into his hair, she closed her fingers, regaining the rains to crush his mouth against her aching tit with a moan, "Mmmm."

The new position had the head of his cock rubbing against her swollen nub. She was desperate for satisfaction.

He anchored her, with one arm reaching down between them, he positioned himself at the entrance of her love duct.

He growled as her impatience drove her down, he sunk into her depth, catching his breath so as not to come. He captured her, restricting her movement.

Chevi's frustration grew like raging bush fire, out of control, she needed to move, she needed to cum. Her hand snaked down to charm her swollen clit into submission, to cajole it into giving her what she wanted, needed, craved.

She teased it gently circling her fingertips around the exposed nerves, growing more and more frenzied as she hungered for release. Her muscles contracting and squeezing their velvet covered cargo, her orgasm exploded through her. She screamed in ecstasy as she saw fireflies dance behind her closed eyes.

Morpheus had reached his threshold. He blinked his eyes and took control. In a shimmer, Chevi was on her knees, with her hands gripping the edge of the tub, he was behind her and buried to the hilt inside her spasming pussy. Her legs spread wide to house his large frame, his weight on one knee as the other cushioned her hip. He pumped her with hard rhythmic strokes that had a second orgasm building with every bump against her cervix, "I wanna feel you cum for me, who do you belong to?" he coerced, as he continued his branding.

This was a taking, a claiming, he was burning her, leaving his mark on her soul. "You, I belong to you," she cried.

"Touch yourself for me, I wanna know when you play with yourself you only ever think of me," he commanded.

She shook her head, "I... I... I can't," she gasped. His hand rose from her hip to make circles on her ass. Her pussy bit down harder on him. He pinched the flesh of her cheek. She reared back, taking him even deeper if that was even possible. He lifted his hand cupped it and slapped her disobedient ass.

"Touch yourself, so I know you will only

ever think of me when you cum." Again he commanded, there were no options when it came to owning this woman. He wanted her body, heart, and most importantly, he needed her mind. He would not lose his dreamwalker to another man, ever.

Her hand rose reluctantly from the edge of the tub. She knew she was about to be bought and paid for. She postponed the transaction by teasing her hardened nipples, pinching and tweaking them.

Again, she felt the burn of his hand as it whipped her backside. She moaned and rolled her hips. Bracing herself on the edge, she lowered her hand to her mound. She slid her two middle fingers between her lips to where their bodies met. Collecting her slippery juices, she slowly tortured her over-sensitive gem.

The water lapping back and forth around their thighs created waves crashing over the rim and onto the tiled floor.

"That's it baby, work it. I wanna feel you cum on my cock. I wanna make you cum as hard as I'm gonna. I'm close," Morpheus felt the tingle from his balls to his scalp, the fire started in his lower back rushing through his prick erupting like a volcano, his hot seed bursting forth like lava. His woman convulsed around him, squeezing every last drop of seed from his soul.

About to collapse backwards onto his haunches, he landed on his bed. Chevi sprawled over him. Both of them struggled to catch their breath. Their throats were burning and dry from exertion.

He rolled them on their sides, kissed her deeply then snuggled her close. He sighed, "I've never met someone as perfect as you."

Chevi laughed, "Well maybe you should wait till you've seen my PMT. You might change your mind."

She smiled and laid her head down on his chest as he started to snore softly.

CHAPTER 16

Zandra stepped out of the shower, "I've already told JT we're going, so you have to speak to your mother and ask her to take Iva for the night. I'm sure she'll jump at the chance to teach her granddaughter some more bad habits."

"Cosmo doesn't consider her influence as bad habits," Destiny laughed at the sight of his curvy wife standing naked with her hands on her hips. She wasn't looking very impressed.

"I'm sorry. I fail to see the funny side of her teaching Iva to draw a door on a wall as funny." She scowled.

"Come on baby, you have to admit it was entertaining to have a room filled with rainforests and butterflies. It could have been worse."

Zandra pushed past him, "Don't defend her. You know Iva is much too young to understand the dangers. All it would take is for her focus on a bad thing and BAM! Look what Iva let in... a ten foot crocodile or wait, even better. What about a demon?" She paused half way across the room, "Hang on, is there such things as demons? If you're a god then demons and stuff must exist... Right?

She stormed to the closet, tossed on some clothes and was pulling the long sleeves up, "You have to help him. He's your brother." With that she left him standing there, naked and chilled.

"Well, I guess we aren't making babies tonight then?" he said under his breath.

He got dressed, went to his library and called his mother. Within seconds, the air around him shifted, and he knew from the fresh gardenia fragrance that she'd arrived.

"You called," she said, sounding as though he was interrupting her life.

"Yes, um... Zandra asked me to see if you would take Iva for a night?" Destiny knew the relationship between the two women was still strained.

"Has she said yes to giving me another grand baby yet?" she asked, her tone still clipped.

"No, not yet. But you never know, she might be persuaded if we could have an evening alone," he countered. He wasn't about to have his mother use Iva as a pawn in a blackmail scheme. He knew how his mother's mind worked.

"Mother, you swore to Zandra that you wouldn't meddle with her reproductive process again, or have you forgotten that?" Destiny stood up for his wife, he would not take the choice away from her. It was a decision they would make together as husband and wife. No matter how much he enjoyed being a father to Iva, it was Zandra's body and that, in the end, trumped everything else.

"Fine, I'll take Iva. But you do whatever it takes to win her over to my side. When is this evening planned?" she inquired, as he handed her the invitation.

Taking it from him she said, "Well, Well what a small world it is?" Then she vanished, leaving Destiny stunned and curious as to what that statement meant.

JT PACED BACK AND FORTH. SHE COULDN'T believe her eyes as she looked at the text from Stephanie. The bitch had quit only days before a huge function. If she was a sook, she would have thrown her phone against the wall and cried. But she was stronger than that and immediately focused on finding a solution.

Stephanie had gone to a rival catering group not because of the money, not because of the hours, but because JT wouldn't sleep with her. In JT's eyes, it wasn't like that. She liked her as a chef for her catering company but that didn't mean she liked her on a personal level, not in that way anyhow.

"Fuck my life." She flopped into the chair, sitting at the desk and she flipped through her compendium. She had three gigs to plan and nobody to prepare the food.

She picked up her phone and re-read the text. This could ruin her. She'd put all her savings into starting up her own business, and with the right people, she knew she could make a comfortable living. She just needed to have faith in herself. "Faith!" She dropped the paperwork and called Zandra.

MORPHEUS FOUND HER, THANKS TO A TWIST of fate and friends in the right place at the right time. He could have kissed his sister-in-law for being the barer of such unbeliev-able luck.

The trouble was, his time was limited, and Destiny had helped him search the li-brary of fate, confirming that his previous attempt to find out about Chevi was a bum steer. It also meant his dreamwalker was ex-actly that, she was meant for him. He just had to convince her of it, without scaring her off.

All the things he wanted to plan and have in place would constantly be interrupted by his female's ability to manipulate his realm, whether awake or asleep.

He was so deep in thought, he didn't even sense Zandra enter his realm until she was standing in the doorway with her hands on her hips and tape measure in hand. "Ahem!" She announced herself.

He frowned, "Does Destiny know you're here?"

"Of course not, don't be silly. He tries to minimize my interaction with the rest of the family. He calls it meddling and reckons your mother does enough of that as it is." She laughed. "On that second part, I have to agree with him."

He smiled, "Indeed, you won't get any argument from me when it comes to analogies of our mother."

.   .   .

"So what brings you here? And what's the tape measure for?" he questioned, eyeing up the scrunched tape in Zandra's hand.

"Well now as I see it, you can either take my help and reward your sister-in-law for being wonderful by giving her a new friend, or you can figure this shit out on your own. Do you have a plan? Coz mines a doozy!" She grinned mischievously.

He thought about it for a minute, summing up how crazy it all sounded, then threw his hands up in surrender. "I'll take all the help I can get." He stood and moved away from the desk.

She made him stick his arms out, turned him this way and that way. If he'd been the same size as Destiny, it would have made things easier but his waist was thinner and he was about an inch shorter. She even made him stand on a piece of paper to draw around his feet, for crying out loud.

"This better be worth it Zandra," he stated.

"Oh quit your fussing, you're being a skirt," she jested.

"Did you just insinuate I was acting like a girl?" His mouth gaped in astonishment.

"If it fits," she laughed.

CHEVI OPENED HER EYES, HER BODY FELT LIKE a big puddle of goo. She'd had two humongous orgasms, her pussy still zinging from the sensation. She'd heard of women having wet dreams, and climaxing while asleep, with the physical intensity strong enough to wake them, but this was ridiculous.

She climbed out of the tub. The water had long gone cold, anyway. She felt ripped off. She wanted the warm body to wrap her afterglow in.

Once dry, she dressed in warm clothes and padded barefoot to the studio. She had three more pieces to do.

She lifted an empty canvas to the easel, and she saw the image in her mind before she picked up her brush. She loaded her pallet with the colors she needed, then began to create. This picture was based on time, she painted an hour glass, an old roman Dias with Roman numerals, a pocket watch on a fob chain, and in the centre, was a shadow of a man. When she finished the mark-up, she put the brushes in solvent, wiped off the pallet and sat it down. A sob escaped her throat. She swiped her hands with a cloth to remove dried paint from her skin, then raised the back of her hand to wipe her nose, sniffled, and became woozy from the residual chemical fumes on her skin. "Stupid bitch," she shook her head to clear it. "Should know better." She chastised herself, switched out the light and went to the bathroom to wash her hands.

She took a couple of tissues from the box on the bench, wiped her eyes, and blew her nose.

Then she went to the kitchen and proceeded to make pancakes with maple syrup, caramelized banana and ice-cream. She put the kettle on to make coffee and walked over to her computer. It had been nearly a week since she'd even checked her emails.

She dished up her plate of food, and with coffee in hand, she sat in front of the screen.

Her first mouthful was bliss, her second and third, pure heaven. She scrolled down her emails to see if anything important had come through on her personal account. She saw one from Olivia and opened it. Attached was a full page spread advertising her show at the gallery. "No pressure, hey Liv?" she muttered to herself.

She suddenly felt the loneliness set in, she missed her dream man. If only he was real, she'd have someone to confide in, someone to offer support. She shivered; someone to keep her warm for fuck sake. Chevi checked her other mail quickly. There was also a 'Thank You' from Harley, saying something about the window getting photographed next week for a tattoo magazine. She sent him a short message of congratulations.

She picked up her half-eaten food, finished her cold coffee and cleaned up.

There really wasn't anything here for her. She was just going through the motions robotically like a machine without emotion. She determined, if she didn't have her art, she'd have nothing.

She picked up her mobile and called her mother, it went to message bank. "Hi mum, just called to say I love you," she said and hung up, then turned her phone to silent. "Well at least it's not off, Olivia." She yawned. It seemed lately she couldn't get enough sleep, and she was forever tired.

She headed for the bedroom, turning lights off on her way. Using the light from the face of her iPhone, she plugged it into the charger and climbed into bed. She'd finish painting the other pieces tomorrow. Tonight she wanted to sleep with her dream lover. She closed her eyes and pictured his face.

ZANDRA HAD AGREED TO LET HER BROTHER-in-law show her something he needed her to do for him. He told her it had to be precise and the quickest and easiest way to do that was for her to close her eyes. He lifted his hand and placed two fingers on her temple. He shut his eyes as well and focused on the image. "Can you see it?" he asked.

"Yes, it's breathtaking. I've never seen anything so spectacular," she replied, scarcely more than a whisper in awe.

Chevi found her lover in the library with his hand on the woman she'd met at the museum. Her jealous rage exploded. She envisioned the woman flying through the air. Then she disappeared before she did any more damage to the woman.

SHE SAT UP IN BED, THREW THE COVERS OFF and stormed back to the studio, more determined than ever to stay awake.

She painted a tear falling from a sad eye and then started on her last piece. She bounced between the others as she waited on each section to dry.

In the past several hours, she had passed through the five stages of grief, some of them more than once. Going in circles, finally she had picked her sanity apart, put it back together and with the heartbreaking truth, she cried for the dream man she'd lost, reminding herself over and over that's all it was. Nothing more than a dream.

"How fucking pathetic. I'm that desperate for a man that I've fallen in love with someone who doesn't even exist outside my own mind." She reprimanded herself, then added, throwing her hands in the air, "Here we go again!"

CHAPTER 17

Morpheus heard a scream that resembled that of a banshee coming from the right. As he opened his eyes, he saw Zandra flying across the room at the hands of his female. It all played out as if it was in slow motion.

Cheval was standing there exuding power, using her energy with force.

Zandra's head hit the wall, landing her on her ass in a most unladylike fashion.

He raised his hand to ask Chevi to stop but before he could speak, she disappeared, taking his heart with her.

He raced to Zandra checking to see that she was alright. Suddenly Destiny appeared in the room standing over him. "What happened?" he demanded.

Morpheus looked at Zandra, his eyes pleading with her not to make it a huge issue.

"Nothing," Zandra told him, "A little misunderstanding, that's all."

Destiny wasn't buying what Zandra was selling, "I felt your fear, don't lie to me," he accused.

"Pull your head in Des. I told you what happened. Take it or leave it." Her husband had a tendency to be overprotective at the best of times. The last thing she needed to do was cause drama between the two brothers. "I'd like to go home now," she finished.

Morpheus reached out his hand to help her up, and Destiny slapped it out of the way like a brat who'd just been roused on.

"I'm fine, a little bruised but not broken. You can take that worried look off your face. Everything's going to work out if we stick to the plan," she winked.

"What plan?" Destiny asked, his eyes glanced from one to the other like he was watching a game of tennis.

Zandra kissed her husband on the cheek and patted his ass. "I'll tell you all about it when we get home."

Destiny took his wife's hand, nodded in his brother's direction, and vanished.

Zandra landed on their bed, "I really hate it when you do that, it makes me dizzy." She sat up, her head spun and she raced for the bathroom, giving up the contents of her stomach to ralph. Her loving husband holding her hair back while she held her conversation with the toilet.

"Are you meddling again?" he asked, after she cleaned herself up and brushed her teeth.

"Maybe I am and maybe I'm not. I see it as 'networking' on a family level." She gave him a lopsided grin before poking her tongue out at him playfully.

His attention immediately drawn to her mouth, "Is that a promise?" He loved the way his wife teased him, she was perfect in his eyes. Her sense of humor kept him on his toes. He found she could lighten his mood just by walking into a room. "Have I told you today how lucky I am, or how much I love you?"

"Well no, come to think of it, I haven't heard a word of it in days and days," she joked.

His arms wrapped around her waist and he pulled her in close. Zandra's mobile phone chose that moment to ring. She pulled it free from her pocket and seeing JT's avatar, she answered it.

JT's voice sped through the ear speaker at a hundred miles an hour. It sounded like a chipmunk overdosed on caffeine.

"Woe, slow it down and take a breath Ms. ADHD. I can't keep up and I missed at least half of that. No, that's a lie, I pretty much missed all of it." Zandra laughed.

"This is not a time for laughing," JT responded. Zandra could almost see her friend with one hand on her hip, her finger pointed in the air and her foot tapping impatiently while waiting for Zandra.

"Zandra, I need you to focus and settle the fuck down. Put your serious face on, I'm dying here," JT cursed. "Everything's gone to shit, all because I wouldn't sleep with the trollop."

"Wait, I'm confused, back it up. What's turned to shit? And who's the trollop? Do I need to hurt someone?" Zandra tapped Destiny on the arm so he'd release her from his bear hug.

He dropped his arms and looked at his wife sympathetically, then indicated with his hand twisting it in front of his mouth, the universal sign for 'Coffee?'

Zandra nodded, then as he made to leave the room, she grabbed his arm, shook her head and again with hand signal, changed it up, 'Wine.'

JT went on to explain her circumstances, how she'd received a text from Stephanie, how she had booking and nobody to cook for any of the functions now. That was when JT dropped Zandra in it, "So you see, I don't have time to look for someone on such short notice, can you ask her? I need to know as soon as possible, and she has to agree to it, I don't care what you have to promise her, pleeeease!" JT begged.

"Okay, okay, breathe. I'll ask her and call

you back. I'll do my best. It's not like I'm a used car salesman or anything," Zandra said, trying to lighten the mood. "Give me a bit, and I'll call you back." She hung up.

She walked to the kitchen, as she entered Destiny, passed her a glass of 'Sweetlips.' She downed it in one hit, passed the empty glass back to him, gave him a kiss, then kissed her daughter in her father's arms. "Wish me luck, duty calls, I'll be back shortly." She then turned and headed down the hall through the door and into the void.

She had no idea how to go about this. She'd only met Faith a handful of times and the woman barely spoke. She clenched her fist knocked and waited.

AFTER FINISHING HER PAINTINGS, CHEVI HAD cleaned her hands, had a shower, made popcorn, played computer games, and rearranged her wardrobe. She cleaned out the fridge and freezer and finally run out of things to keep herself busy enough to stop her from falling asleep. It'd been nearly twenty-four hours since she dozed off and witnessed Sandy touching that Zandra woman. She wasn't counting the previous hours. The idea was to keep moving every time she felt herself start to nod off. She got up walked around and started a new task.

She put a Pilate's disc in the DVD player and turned on the TV, but settled for playing Wii-fit instead. After going through all the different challenges, she was fucked.

Chevi sat down on the couch and flicked through the channels to see what was on free to air. 'Utter crap!' She couldn't find anything worth watching, so she switched it off.

She started to read a novel on her iPhone, her eyes growing heavy, she found herself reading the same paragraph two and three times before finally, simultaneously her hand dropped and her head lolled against the cushion.

A knock at the door saved her just as she was falling asleep. She jumped up and raced to answer it. Looking through the peep-hole she identified a delivery man, "Who is it?" She called out, always cautious.

"Courier, I have a delivery for Cheval Noland, I need a signature, ma'am," the delivery guy called through the timber barrier.

She swung the door open, signed her name with a scribble on his electronic pad, and took possession of the parcels and box.

Baffled as to what could be inside, she carried them awkwardly to the dining room and laid them on the table. When she lifted the smaller parcel off the top, she found an envelope stuck to the lid, her hand shook as she reached for it. She removed it from the tape holding it in place and flipped it over to see the reverse side was as blank as its front. Slipping a nail under the edge she opened it, sliding the card out, she read.

'DREAMING OF YOU ALWAYS'
   L&Xxxz DMS

SHE STARED AT THE CARD DUMBFOUNDED, 'Who the fuck is DMS,' she wondered. Maybe it was one of the private benefactors from the gallery. Olivia had said she often gave advanced private viewings to some of her more eccentric clientele.

She shrugged and put the card down on the table. Still as baffled about it all, she lifted the lid on the large white package, peeled back the white tissue paper and saw the most spectacular tones of red so dark they were almost black. Her stomach dropped like someone had cut the cables on her elevator of life. Her heart raced, it wasn't just any dress it was the dress. The one she'd seen in her dream. "Oh my fucking god," she mumbled as she pulled the lid off the second one, "What the fuck is going on here?" she said, as she lifted the paper cover, staring at a pair of elegant gold shoes. It was an eerie feeling to see them marked with her size. She replaced the lids exactly how she'd received them, took them to her bedroom and stored them under her bed.

She then raced to the kitchen and made a coffee. Out of sight did not mean out of mind. Was her dream prophetic? She returned to her computer and hit the spacebar to wake it up. She then typed into the search engine, Dreams and pressed enter. She sat reading anything she could find. Her tired eyes glanced over yet another useless page of results. As she scrolled down to the bottom, she caught sight of one word that stood out 'Dreamwalker.' She hit the link. It took her to a page that described it as a person who could dream so vividly, it was hard to distinguish between what was real and what was a dream fabrication. There was a story about a little girl whose dreams were so realistic that she was convinced that what she did while asleep were actually things she'd done in real life. She'd dreamt of ice-skating on the weekend at a friend's place, yet she'd spent the weekend at home. Convinced that it would resolve the confusion, her parents had taken her to an ice-skating rink. The girl took to the ice like a professional even though she'd never skated before.

She got lost in her fact-finding mission, intrigued by the thought that someone could actually control their dreams. It also explained a lot about her experiences as a teenager.

~

MORPHEUS WAS NOW SLIGHTLY MORE CRAZY than he'd been in previous weeks. It felt like he hadn't seen his female in forever. He kept playing in his mind the enraged look of hurt on her face. She'd obviously thought he was being unfaithful. He'd searched time and time again for her in his mind but hadn't managed to find her.

When he checked on Zandra to see if she was okay, she told him she'd taken care of his request. She'd collected his things and passed them on to him. Along with the tux and shoes, she gave him a mobile phone.

She assured him that everything was on schedule for tomorrow night. Then shooed him out the door so to speak, cutting the visit short.

She said, "Everything will be fine, but I have to check on Faith." So he'd left her to it.

~

FAITH WAS IN HER KITCHEN hyperventilating, she'd only ever cooked for her family and they were only a select few. She kept telling herself she could do this, she just needed to have faith in herself. Now that was a joke. She had lost her faith a long time ago. Could she find it in herself to pull it together and make this work... just this once?

She took a caramel pie from the fridge, grabbed a fork from the drawer, and proceeded to eat nearly half the damn thing in one sitting. She looked down and swore, "Fuck me," she rolled her eyes. Guilty, she covered the remains, then went about making another. Megan had apparently been craving caramel tart, and now she'd gone and stress eaten it on her. It wasn't very comforting. She supposed it was because it wasn't hers to be comforted by. It was a very pregnant Megan's.

Destruction had beaten down her door at some stupid hour in the middle of the night, saying Megan had one of her cravings going on.

She was rather honored that her big brother came straight to her. She liked Megan and Zandra too. But she didn't want to get too familiar with them; humans always seemed to disappoint her in the end.

"Oh fuck it," she said as she waved her hand over the dish. One minute she was looking at a pile of ingredients on the bench and the next, there was a scrumptious caramel pie in its place. She didn't feel like cooking, for the first time in forever.

She scooped it up off the bench and went knocking on her brother's door.

Destruction answered it, "Hey sis, come on in,"

"No thanks. I have things I have to take care of. Can you apologize to Megan for taking so long," she said looking at her bare feet.

Megan's heavily pregnant frame emerged from the bedroom down the hall, she looked pale and her sweats were smeared with something dark. "D..." She doubled over in pain.

He dropped the dish his sister had given him and raced to her side, "What's wrong? What's happening?"

"Call an ambulance, something's not

right," She panted through another stab in her lower abdomen.

"Faith, I need you to get my phone. It's on the side table, now!" Destruction demanded.

She jumped over the broken pie, and ran to where she'd been instructed, snatched up the phone and delivered it to his hand. He was now on the floor holding his beloved wife. He looked as pale and scared as she was.

Destruction dialed 911, he then spoke to the responding person on the other end of the call. "No, yes," he rattled off the address. He soothed his worried Megan saying, "Hang in there, they're coming baby, you stay with me Megan, don't you dare leave me."

She held up her hand to show she still wore her ring. He took her hand and gently brought it to his lips then kissed it, "I never take it off, I'm a part of you and you're a part of me. I love you," she then passed out.

"Fuck!" He ran his hand through his hair, only then realizing he was still connected to the emergency operator. He returned the phone to his ear and informed them that Megan was now unconscious. As he could hear sirens approaching from the front of the house, he turned to Faith, "Can you let Zandra know what's going on? And there's a bag in there at the foot of the walk-in-robe, she's going to need that."

Faith gathered the bag and brought it to his side, he then asked, "Can you open the front door and let them in?"

She looked in the direction, then back at her brother, he didn't know, she'd never told anyone. As she moved to follow his instructions, the walls wavered, like they were waterfalls covered in running water. Her breathing became heavy, her feet felt like lead. She braced one wall with an outstretched hand to steady herself. All she could hear was a loud buzzing sound in her ears.

She kept telling herself "I can do this, I have to do this." Over and over, she chanted her mantra step by step, her hands finally landed on the door. She took two big breaths and opened it, as her eyes caught sight of the world on the other side, the color drained out of it and she thought she was going to pass out. She clung to the knob, but it was no good, she went down like a sack of potatoes without enough warning to zap herself back to her realm.

Destruction lifted his head and saw his sister fall but there wasn't anything he could do for her, she'd live. One of the EMT's made her way to Megan, and the other attended to his sister. He couldn't say anything about Faith being a god. Both women were bundled up and in the back of the ambulance within minutes. He then reached for his phone and called Destiny to let him know Megan would need Zandra at the hospital. As he hung up, the EMT attending to Megan explained that her vital signs were good and that she could hear a heartbeat, she asked, "When is she due?"

Destruction gave answers before the question was finished, "She's thirty-six weeks," his mind registering that she had only mentioned a heartbeat not two. "She's, I mean, we're having twins."

The EMT nodded, like she knew what he was asking, she went back to Megan's belly, then said, "She seems to be having contractions, has she had any high blood pressure?"

He explained about the doctor placing her on bed rest for the past few weeks, he'd said something about pre-eclampsia. She'd only been allowed the luxury of the bathroom to shower and to use the toilet.

He'd been her constant doting husband the entire time. He held her hand as the siren screaming vehicle made its way to the nearest hospital. They'd known at the end of the first trimester, that because she was having twins and because of their size, Megan would be robbed of having a home birth. They didn't care, so long as all of them were healthy.

As a god, he felt helpless. He wished he could do something to help, to make this alright. He called out to his mother in his mind, telling her what was happening.

He felt a warm glow on his cheek and words whispered back to him in his mother's voice, "What will be, will be my son. Have faith."

His eyes flew to his sister's form, out

cold on the other stretcher, "How can I have faith, when she's unconscious?"

~

DESTINY YELLED TO HIS WIFE FROM THE kitchen, moving as fast as possible to reach her in Iva's room, "Megan's on her way to the hospital, something's wrong. We need to go. I'll pack some things for Iva and we'll meet at the car."

Zandra lifted Iva up to her hip, and raced to grab her bag with a change of clothes, spare nappies and bum wipes. She patted the pocket of her jeans to check she had her phone. She'd call JT once they were on their way.

She knew JT would have her hands full with the gallery preparations but she also knew that her best friend would help out with Iva if needed.

The three women had become quite the force to be reckoned with although it was hard to do much with Megan on bed rest and JT starting her new business venture.

She put Iva into the car seat and buckled

her in, then turned to collect the stuff Destiny had put together and added them to Iva's bag. She stepped back, shut the door, and climbed into the passenger seat. She was in no state to drive. Destiny started the car and reversed out. As he drove, Zandra called JT to let her know what was happening.

She then sent a text message to Vanessa, updating her as to Megan's situation. She knew no matter where she was she'd want to know. Since delivering her Iva, she'd been in contact with her a few times via text. Destiny knew they had stayed in touch but he didn't want to know about the details. He didn't want to lie to his brother if asked. Technically he had no idea about anything. Zandra had asked him to keep it that way at Vanessa's request.

Her phone buzzed with a responding text from Vanessa almost instantly, saying she'd just settled into her new place, and asking which hospital.

VANESSA HEARD HER PHONE BEEP WITH THE name of the hospital. She was in a mixed mind about what to do, she was drawn to the comradery of Megan, Zandra and JT, but could she risk Death being there? It was a hospital and his family. The chances were high, she played his words over in her mind, "One day, I'll make you stop running from me," her heart sped up at the replayed threat.

The drive was about an hour, and if she was careful, she could hide. She raced to the bedroom of her small apartment, quickly dressed, then pulled a wig down from the top of the cupboard.

CHAPTER 18

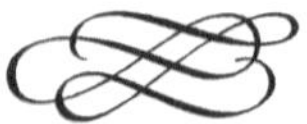

As the EMT's wheeled Megan into the ER, they were met by doctors and nurses. After a quick examination, Megan was raced off to surgery for an emergency C-section. Destruction was told to stay on the other side of the now swinging doors.

He stared numbly at them, as he watched his entire existence, his world get wheeled into an operating theatre. He saw his brother through the clear glass as they swung, there one minute, gone the next. Nobody else would be able to see Death. He wasn't in solid form.

His stomach dropped and his fear spiked. Was his brother here to take from him what was his? Death was on the other side, in the vicinity of his Megan and their soon to be born infants.

He checked over his shoulder, there were too many people around. He needed a secluded place for what he planned to do. Observing his surroundings, he made his way to the fire escape.

With his back against the door, he summoned his energy, the concrete under his boots cracked. "Aargh!" He yelled in frustration, for him to become invisible would unleash his powers. Troy would unleash Destruction. The possibility that he could disintegrate the entire hospital into a pile of rubble around his loved ones stopped him. He abandoned his attempts to go after Death. His mother's words played in his mind again, 'What will be, will be.'

He still couldn't decipher whether Cosmo meant it as a warning, a foreboding of something bad.

He took a steadying breath and turned, as his hand twisted the knob, he felt the presence behind him. He snarled, "Why are you here?" He knew if the security guards were watching the cameras in the fire escape, all they would see was him talking to himself, like any normal stressed out person with a sick or dying loved one. Death didn't answer. He just placed a concerned hand on Des's shoulder. Troy shrugged it off then barked, "Tell me, Why are you here?" he demanded.

Death had been drawn to the hospital, he didn't know why exactly. How was he supposed to explain that kind of instinct to his brother as he worried about his wife and babies?

He ran his fingers through his hair, wanting to tug it out in frustration. He sighed, "I don't know, alright! I just sensed I had to be here." He waved his hands to annunciate his words.

Death could see the evidence in Destruction's eyes. If his brother could hit him right now he would. Troy's nostrils flared and his eyes glazed over with hatred.

Death raised his hands in surrender, "I'm pretty sure I'm not here because of Megan or the twins," he said, crossing his fingers. "Mother told me to come." His intention was to reassure Destruction, but when you're the personification of death, there's not much you could say or do that would bring comfort.

DESTINY AND ZANDRA ENTERED THE hospital. They looked around for Destruction but couldn't see him. "Send him a text to let him know we're here," Zandra suggested.

Des shuffled Iva from one arm to the other, so he could access his phone, then tapped in the message and hit send. He hoped his brother had his phone on him and it wasn't switched off. They made their way to the chairs in the reception area to wait.

VANESSA HAD BEEN RIDING AT THE designated speed. She'd always been a careful driver, no matter what the mode of transport.

She had ditched the car she'd used the last few years, it'd been time to update, anyway. She hadn't ridden a motorbike in a while, but it was like the pair were inseparable. It made for a fast getaway if she needed it. And Death knew her old car on sight. It made it too easy for him to follow her.

She parked her wheels underground in the hospital's car park, then removed her gloves and helmet. She pulled at the wig gently to ensure it was securely in place. She threw her bag over her shoulder and locked her helmet in the side-saddle.

Standing with her hands on her hips, she shook her head thinking 'I must be crazy.' Her gut was telling her this was a bad idea. Her heart was racing as she walked up to the elevator and pushed the button.

ZANDRA GAVE OUT A LOW WHISTLE AS SHE watched the elevator doors open. A sexy blonde with curves swaggered out in black leathers, wearing dark sunglasses. Damn, what she wouldn't give to rock that look.

The woman strode straight up to her. Zandra laughed, "Oh My Fucking God! Vanessa?"

Vanessa lifted her sunnies briefly to show her full face with a smirk. "None other," she replied.

"Love the new look, but do you really think it's enough to keep you safe?" Zandra doubted her friend's confidence in her attempt to hide.

Zandra saw Destiny turn his head in her peripheral vision. Next thing, Iva was passed off to her, and he was on the move. Everything seemed to be moving in slow motion. In the blink of an eye, Death had appeared in the doorway behind Troy and he looked pissed.

He pushed Destiny out of the way and stormed up to Vanessa. He placed his arm around her waist and spun her on her heels. She lost her footing and landed in his embrace, with surprise. He captured her lips as she tried to fight him off, then with no regard for the laws they lived by, they vanished.

Zandra jumped up, "Shit, shit, do something Des, he took her, she wasn't ready yet. Do something. You have to help her."

Des reached Zandra and held both of his girls to reassure them everything would be alright. "I'm sorry Zan. There's nothing I or anyone else can do for her now. It's between her and Death."

It may have sounded callus, but Troy was glad that his brother was gone and otherwise occupied, even if it was at Vanessa's expense. His Megan would be upset about it when she found out but they had bigger things to worry about.

He felt the shaky hand on his arm and the small voice speaking to him, "Congratulations sir, you have two healthy babies, a boy and a girl. Your wife is doing well, and they'll be taking her down the hall to recovery shortly. If you'd like to see them, you can follow me."

"Fuck!" His knees were weak, and he needed a minute to compose himself. He turned to his family and did a thumbs-up signal to indicate all was well, "We have a boy and a girl," he said, once he was sure his voice wouldn't break from the emotions that coursed through him.

As he went to leave the room, he suddenly remembered his sister, "Fuck! Des, Faith is here somewhere. Can you find her?"

Zandra had walked off to meet JT at the entrance, but had been listening to what transpired between her husband and brother-in-law.

She took JT's hand saying, "Come on, we need to find your cook, and my sister-in-law. She still hasn't given me an answer I'm happy with."

She passed Iva to Des on the way past, kissed his cheek and said, "I've got this one. Can you take Iva home? I'll see you soon."

Des smiled, "If you're sure? We'll see you back at the house."

Cheval pulled the box from under her bed and sat with it in front of her. She held a coin in her hand. Heads, I wear the dress, tails, it stays under the bed.

She flipped the coin into the air, caught it and slapped it on the back of her hand.

She shivered from a weird feeling of being watched. She looked around, then at the coin toss, 'Heads' her heart raced, "Guess I'm wearing the damn dress," she said as she tossed the coin into the bedside drawer. She didn't even see it land, but Cosmo knew eventually Chevi would find the two-headed coin and realize she'd been played.

Cosmo liked Chevi for her son. She knew he'd be safe with her, and would find peace in her arms.

CHAPTER 19

Morpheus closed his eyes to return to his duties. He heard his sister scream, he rarely invaded his siblings' dreams. He felt he wouldn't like it if the tables were turned and they involved themselves in his affairs, so he avoided them. He couldn't ignore Faith though, she sounded like she was in trouble.

He zoomed in on the fine thread that led him to her, she was in a hospital, on a bed, screaming, only stopping long enough to suck in another full breath of fresh air. She was frantically gripping the rails, crying out, "No! No! Take me home, I don't want to be here, I can't be here." Her lids flashed open, and she locked eyes with Morpheus, "Help me brother, don't leave me here. Please?"

He walked to the side of her bed and placed a hand to her forehead to sooth her. "Shhhh, little one, it's only a dream."

"No, it's not, they took me. You have to come and get me. I'm at the hospital where Megan and Troy are. I'm too messed up to get home on my own, my powers won't work here."

Just as the dream started to fade, Morpheus could hear Zandra's voice, "Faith, sweetie can you hear me? We've come to take you home, but I need you to open your eyes for me. Faith?"

Morpheus called to Faith, "You're safe now, go to Zandra, follow her voice. She'll help you. You can trust her."

Faith tried to reach out for her brother but he was gone. She could feel someone holding her hand. She opened her eyes and saw the most intensely blue-green eyes she'd ever seen looking back at her. She became lost in their beauty for a moment, then realized they were attached to a face that didn't belong to Zandra.

"Shhhh, you're okay. We've got you. This is my friend JT. JT, this is my sister-in-law Faith."

JT moved to release Faith's hand, "Awkward! Sorry, you were waving your hands around and we didn't want you to hurt yourself." Faith gripped JT's hand firmer, not wanting her to let go. She almost felt calm, almost. Considering she was in the outside.

"So I hear you're an amazing cook? I know this is putting you on the spot but I'm desperate. Any chance we could get out of here and grab a coffee and maybe something sweet to bring your sugars back up." JT was working on the theory that distraction was always a handy tool.

Faith's heart was racing, and for the first time in forever, she wanted to get to know a human. She found herself nodding, "Oh, but wait!" She said, "I can't go out there, not where the other humans are." She whispered conspiratorially, her nodding head now shaking side to side.

Zandra and JT looked at each other, not sure what to say or do.

~

Morpheus paused in his mind, remembering Cheval's nightmare that he'd inhaled. Maybe now that he had a little information about who and what she was, he could analyze it more fully.

His mind coughed up the murky sludge of smoke. He ran at it full force leaping into the centre as it swallowed him whole. It prickled his skin zapping him with electricity. As he stood and turned around to see where he was, he recognized his surrounding to be a hospital. There were subtle differences that he associated with an asylum. He'd often played in places like this, when overridden with boredom. Some of the medication they pumped into their humans made for interesting diversions from his normal fodder.

He looked through the window in the door closest to him. There, restrained to a bed was a much younger version of his female Cheval. She was crying in her sleep.

His heart went out to the cruelty of her situation. He watched in amazement as she somehow managed to separate from her body and undo the restraints. Her tiny body sat up and climbed out of the bed. She walked to the door and waited. The free spirit of Cheval vanished through the wall beside the steel door and suddenly reappeared next to him on this side of the wall. As she emerged from the plaster, she looked straight at him, her eyes grew wide for a moment, but she continued on her path, regardless. She placed a hand on his arm and pushed him back out of the way. Now without him blocking the door to the room, her small hand could reach for the handle and unlock it. She pulled the door open, swinging it so wide that it hit the wall leaving a mark. The solid body of Cheval walked through the open door and stopped. Her long, brown hair covered her face, but Morpheus could tell her eyes were still closed, with tears still streaking down her juvenile face, as teardrops landed on the grey linoleum floor.

The ghost-like apparition of his little Chevi stepped up to the sleepwalker and submerged its form. They reconnected. The young human gasped, then laughed with glee as she opened her eyes and raised her haunting chocolate color of them to stare in confusion at him. "Who are you?" she asked.

"I'm just a dream," he said. He felt as though he was invading her privacy by being here, but he didn't understand how this dream was something Chevi feared.

From the end of the corridor, a fat, balding man started toward them, as he looked past his immature female toward the approaching man. Chevi turned to look over her shoulder. She ran to seek shelter behind him. Trying to hide, crying out, "No, No, No, don't let him take me, I don't wanna go back. I'll be good, I promise. Please?"

The man walked straight through Morpheus and grabbed Chevi by the arm, no matter how much she kicked and screamed, as he manhandled her back into the room.

He threw her forcefully onto the bed, strapped her hands tightly back into the restraints, then pulled a syringe from his pocket and jabbed it into her thigh. She let out one final cry, "No....!" Her bladder released, wetting herself as she passed out cold. He left her there with her hospital gown only half covering her shivering and vulnerable body. He didn't even cover her with a sheet or blanket to stave off the cold.

Morpheus was furious and disgusted. His female had been drugged, terrorized and humiliated.

CHEVI HAD A SHOWER, AND FOUND THAT because she was so sleep-deprived, she was finding it hard to breathe. She climbed into bed convincing herself she wasn't going to dream about her dream lover tonight. She sunk into dreamland as soon as her eyes were closed. This time her dream was random, a borderline nightmare. She was too tired to wake up and too exhausted to manipulate and change the scene. She was swallowed by the vision. She found herself in a hostel, surrounded by elderly people. It clicked in her mind she was in an old persons' nursing home, she became anxious to see why her dreams had brought her here. She walked down the hall. As she made her way to the end, she'd glanced through the open doors not recognizing any of the faces that looked back at her as she passed by. She reached the last room on the right and froze.

Sitting in a chair was someone she knew, she'd never forget that face. Even older, his features were unmistakable. Her heart raced and for a second she was fifteen again. Her eyes were fixed on the shell of a man. Her head shaking sideways, 'No... I don't want to go back. Please don't take me back.' She heard herself begging, she jumped as strong arms wrapped around her from behind.

"You're safe, this is not your dream my love." Morpheus whispered next to her ear.

She choked on her breath as she gasped for air, her panic slowly settling. "Why am I here?" she asked.

"I wanted to show you that time catches up with all evil, eventually. Just watch," Morpheus said. He was not about to let his woman miss out on seeing what had become of her abuser.

A male nurse walked into the room, he showed no care for the old man. He wrapped a sling around his upper body and used a remote to lift the almost dead weight into the bed, with no regard for the straps that dug into flesh, biting and pinching the fragile skin under his arms. He didn't speak to him. He flitted around taking blood pressure and temperature, then jotted it down on a chart.

He drew a needle from his pocket and injected the old man in the thigh. The old man whimpered as it was roughly administered. He was unconscious when the nurse stepped away from obstructing their view.

The man's breathing was shallow, he had spittle dribbling down his cheek and his pajama pants showed he'd wet himself. The nurse walked out of the room past them, not seeing them, completely unaware of the presence.

She watched for another minute before saying, "I don't want to see anymore, I've seen enough."

"I just wanted you to see, your nightmares can't hurt you anymore. He will soon pass over. He can no longer touch you." He rested his chin on the top of her head,

"You're safe with me, and I'm safe with you. Please don't leave me. I need you more than you need me."

The dream faded away, and she woke to find she had one more painting she needed to complete before tonight. She jumped out of bed and raced to throw some clothes on. She didn't even look at the clock, she didn't have time.

CHAPTER 20

Destruction sat waiting for the love of his life to wake up. His Megan had been placed in a private room. The nurses had been in to check on her several times. They'd also explained to him, she'd been through a lot and that her body needed the sleep. The more rest she could have, the faster she would recover, but he felt helpless.

"I'll feel much better when she wakes up for more than a few minutes at a time. At the moment, I'm too scared to touch her," he'd told one of the nurses.

After he was certain they were alone, he

called out to his mother. When she appeared in the corner of the room like a ghost, he demanded, "I need you to heal her, to take the pain away."

"Son, I love you but you don't understand what you are asking me to do," she said sadly. "Childbirth isn't as glorious as people think. It's painful even with the easiest labor."

"Then give me her pain. I'll carry it for her. She's earned that much. I love her with all that I am, and if I can make this burden less traumatic, then she won't be scared by it. Please let me do this for her."

"Alright." Cosmo gave in to her son's request. She waved her hands over Megan's sleeping form, then moved to her son and did the same.

He sunk to his knees, and cried out, "Aargh!" as his body felt like it had been torn open, every movement left him wincing with the sting of deep tissue bruises and severed muscle.

Cosmo smiled at her son, and said in a superior voice, "That is why woman will always be the stronger gender."

FAITH HAD NO IDEA HOW SHE HAD MADE IT back to Zandra's. All she knew was if JT hadn't kept her talking the entire time, she would probably still be in that hospital cubicle-like room, screaming her lungs out.

She couldn't explain the unbelievable feeling of inner peace that filled her, at just the brush of a knee against JT's.

She had even inadvertently agreed to help JT out with the catering for the exhibition at a gallery which was why she was racing around trying to get ready now. She'd finished all the preparation and everything looked great. JT was due to pick up the many trays of food from Zandra's in about fifteen minutes. She was so nervous about presenting the canapés that she felt raw.

Her nerves getting the better of her, she excused herself and made her way back to her place to freshen up.

CHEVI PLUCKED HER EYEBROWS, THEN SHAVED her legs quickly. She then sporadically threw hot rollers into her hair. After which she swore and cursed at herself, 'Well, that was fucking daft' she looked at the shower. She should have waited until after to put the hot rollers in. Instead she opted for a hot bath, to avoid having to get her hair wet.

She was nervous about tonight, she wasn't sure if she would pull it off. She really needed to sell all the paintings to make things a little easier over the next month while she waited for more commission assignments to flow in. The hard part was having to turn some down to free up the time to prepare for nights like tonight.

She sped through her bath, then climbed out, dried herself off and then wrapped in a towel, she applied a light shading of makeup. Once she was satisfied, she removed the hot rollers and began to tastefully pin up the large bouncy curls. She was flying blind on most of it, but with a twist here and there she managed to mimic the image she'd seen of her hair at the gallery through Sandy's eyes.

She stepped into the bedroom and admired the dress laid out ready to slip on. She had decided that because of the cut and design of the dress she wouldn't be able to wear a bra, she was not going anywhere without underwear though. She pointed her toes as she stepped into a G-string, then wiggled her bum as she pulled them up. With the thin scrap of white lace in place, she felt sexy.

She raced to the bathroom and rifled through the drawer to find the perfect nail polish, she decided to go for a clear shine, as she thought any other color would look gaudy. Her hands shook as she painted it on her nails. Chevi then waved her hands back and forth blowing on them to try to speed up the drying process. Because that was taking too long, she hit them one at a time with the cold shot of her blow-dryer.

She stepped back into the bedroom and proceeded to scrunch up her stockings one at a time, sliding them up her legs. Once the elastic was in place around her mid-thigh, she glanced in the mirror. With the lace panties covering her snatch she thought to herself 'that's hot', but with the stocking added to the equation she felt all 'hellfire woman.'

"I'd do me," she said to herself, with a satisfied smile.

She lifted the gorgeous gown from where it had been laying on the bed and stepped into it. The fabric was smooth and slinky on her skin. For the first time in her life she felt elegant. And as she turned in front of the mirror, she didn't even give a shit if people saw her tattoos on her exposed back.

MORPHEUS WAITED PATIENTLY UNTIL THE last minute. He lifted a pouch of dream sand from his desk drawer and placed it carefully in his pocket. He was seconds from walking out the door when the room shifted and he caught the scent of gardenia. "Mother, I'm kind of busy. Can this wait till another time?"

He turned to face Cosmo and found her standing with Iva on her hip, "Do you wish to claim your Cheval tonight, to bring her home?" she asked as she cupped Iva's head and kissed the top of it.

Morpheus looked at his mother as though she wasn't to be trusted, then answered, "Yes, why do you ask?"

"Good, you need to give her this," she held out her palm, which contained an intricately carved box. "This, if she chooses, will bring you both together forever. The happiness is yours and hers for the making. You can plan your retirement from this realm, together."

Morpheus slipped the box into his other pocket. "The choice is entirely up to her, but I'll be playing for keeps. Thank you, Mother. I really need to get going," he informed her.

She gave a curt nod of her head before whispering to her granddaughter, "Let's go and see what mischief we can find, little one." They both vanished with mischievous giggles ringing through the air. He gave a moment's thought to his mother's behavior around his niece. They were definitely cut from the same cloth.

He wondered if one day he would see his

love for Chevi grow inside her belly. He smiled at the thought of seeing her body swell and grow full with his child. But he didn't have time to waste. He pulled the cell phone from his pocket that Zandra had given him and sent the text message to start the next stage of his plan, well, her plan really.

CHEVI APPLIED A DARK BLOOD RED LIPSTICK and checked her appearance one last time in the mirror. She'd managed to find a gold clutch purse that was close enough to her sandals in color and it would be far enough away from them to make it work.

She checked the locks on all the windows, snatched up her keys and phone and placed them along with some money into her purse. She hoped it wouldn't get too cold tonight as she didn't have a shawl to keep warm and nothing in her closet matched.

She pulled the door closed, locking it behind herself. She turned to find a gentleman standing at the bottom of the steps. "Miss Noland, I'll be your driver for this evening," he informed her.

187

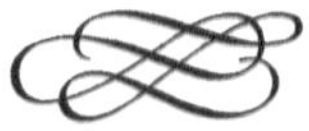

Chevi was surprised to find Olivia had gone to such extremes as to have a limo pick her up. She hadn't expected that.

The driver opened the back door of the limo and offered her a hand to steady her as she slid into the back seat. She watched him closely as he closed the door, distracted by his good looks that somehow seemed familiar, that she didn't realize she wasn't alone. A slight movement from the other side of the vehicle caused her to jump.

"Oh, I'm sorry I didn't mean to startle you," a female's voice informed her as a face leaned into the light.

The fairytale abruptly burst, as she recognized her dream nemesis, Zandra.

"I'm sorry. I don't understand?" She suddenly felt awkward, and the spacious rear area of the limo became instantaneously claustrophobic.

"Oh, I guess Olivia forgot to mention that we offered to pick you up. This way you can have a couple of glasses of champagne and not worry about driving home, especially on such a big night." Zandra exaggerated the truth to suit her plans.

"Thank you so much, that's very kind of you." She gave a forced smile that she hoped didn't resemble a snarl, then chastised herself mentally, 'It was a fucking dream, you dumbass. You can't hold it against a real live person.'

Tonight would top the scale at spectacular that was for sure. She was hoping tonight's event would make her career. She wasn't sure who Zandra was exactly, but she was in her limo and the woman was dressed elegantly in a black evening dress.

~

Destiny slid into the driver's seat, and turned the ignition key, he still had no idea how he had been bamboozled into Zandra's grand scheme of things. He chuckled to himself as he pulled the car back towards the gallery. He knew exactly how she'd used her powers of persuasion, but he'd fought the good fight and won, he'd had his own agenda. At the prime moment, he had provided his own valid argument by holding back Zandra's orgasm; only when she'd agreed to his terms of the arrangement had he taken them both to climax. He'd given in to her hair-brained ideas and she'd given in to his, by the end of the night. If he had anything to do about it she would be pregnant if she wasn't already.

As the car travelled to the event, Chevi made small talk with Zandra, neither paying that much attention to street lights as they flickered to life or the topic of conversation.

She was off in her own little world. She wished she was sharing the last few minutes with her dream man, sharing tonight with him. She'd been thinking about it long and hard and had come to the decision that she was keeping the painting of her dream man.

As the door opened in front of the red carpet that had been rolled out at the entry, she thanked Zandra for picking her up, then made an excuse to speak to Olivia privately before the other guests started to arrive.

She almost ran headlong into Olivia as she was giving instructions to a staff member. She patiently waited for her to finish before moving closer to whisper, "Can I speak to you in your office?"

Olivia's face lit up instantly, "Of course, I have something for you. It arrived today. I'm can't wait to see what's in it." Olivia took her hand as she lifted the skirting on her evening gown.

She was pulled along by Olivia like she was in a school yard chase.

They stepped into the office and Olivia quickly closed the door behind them. Then rushed to the safe, punching in a digital security code, Olivia cranked the handle to crack it open. Chevi watched as her friend's reaching hands shook, withdrawing a large black velvet box.

She could see there was a small envelope pinned to the top of the box as Olivia sat it on her desk to close the safe.

"Quick! Quick! Open it. I'm dying to see what's inside it, I've been waiting four and a half hours since it arrived and I can't take it anymore, put me out of my misery. Please?"

Chevi's heart raced as she ran her fingers over the black velvet, she pulled the blank envelope free of its pin and slid the card out.

MAY ALL YOUR HOPES AND DREAMS COME **true tonight.**

L&xxxz DMS

· · ·

THE CARD SLIPPED FROM HER FINGERS AS SHE passed it to Olivia and sat down hard on the chair in front of the desk.

Olivia retrieved the note and after reading it asked her, "Who is DMS?"

"I don't know. I was going to ask you if you knew who it was. I received a delivery the other day, and I was wondering if it was one of your more eccentric customers."

"No, I haven't had to do a pre-show for anyone, but that's because the entire collection has been sold already."

"What? No it can't be. I was going to speak to you about keeping the masterpiece of the collection."

"I'm sorry Chevi, but I couldn't refuse the sale, and he was quite adamant that he wanted the complete collection. Darling, tonight is your night. It's a night of celebration. Now are you going to open that thing or am I? We need to get out there, people will be arriving very soon." Olivia beamed.

"Alright, let's do this." Chevi said, rubbing her fingertips around the edge, she cracked the wax seal on the ribbon connecting the lid to its base. Her left hand held it steady while her right thumb lifted the lid to reveal a spectacular necklace, bracelet and matching earrings.

Chevi's comment was lost on Olivia, "Oh my fucking god!" It was the gold encrusted gems from her dream.

Olivia pounced on them while Chevi sat there lost in her shocked confusion. Within a couple of minutes, she was donned in all their glory. "There now, that was definitely worth all the excitement." Olivia said as she stepped back to admire Chevi's beauty.

"Wow! Just wow! That's all I can say. Oh have you got room inside that little gold purse to put your check?" Olivia asked as she passed an envelope to her.

She graciously took the envelope and folded it in half then stuffed it unceremoniously into her purse. She'd look at it later, for now she just had to suck it up and get through the tonight. She felt worn out and drained. Chevi wanted to go home, her thoughts of her masterpiece never being seen again after the close of the gallery at the end of the function made her eyes sting with unshed tears. She fanned her face with her free hand, took a breath in and blew it out slowly. She sniffled as she took a tissue from the desktop holder. "I can do this, it's only a couple of hours," she told herself.

Olivia thought Chevi was talking to her so she responded with encouragement, "Yes you can. Now go use the powder room and freshen up, I'll meet you out front. Okay?"

Chevi gave a nod. She knew her voice would crack and the tears would spill smearing her make-up if she spoke. She stepped around Olivia and made her way to the ladies' room.

There she took several more calming breaths and attended to her teary eyes in the mirror. Once satisfied that the crisis had been averted, she stepped back and for the first time since stepping into the small space looked at herself as a whole in the mirror. She was stunning, just like her dream man had shown her.

She paused with her hand on the door handle, pushed her shoulders back and entered the fray.

Olivia met her with applause as she entered the room, drawing attention to her appearance amongst the guests. A waiter moved forward with a tray of champagne glasses, she took two flutes and passed one to Chevi. "If I can have everyone's attention for a moment please, I'd like to introduce you all to the lady of the night, Ms. Cheval Noland. I'd like you all to raise your glasses in a toast, may she have a long and prosperous career."

Chevi lifted her own glass to salute the room full of elegantly dressed men and women, smiled and somehow managed to refrain from downing the entire glass in one hit, instead sipping it in a ladylike fashion.

Olivia leaned in close and whispered in her ear, "I'm not going to announce just yet that the entire collection has already sold. We will wait a little while, we want to see how much business we can drum up. Now, go mingle."

Chevi spent the next half an hour doing as she was told while drinking champagne and eating delicious little bites of food and canapés.

She stood in front of her masterpiece with an empty glass, lost in her thoughts, miserable about the loss of it, when a waiter tapped her on the shoulder. She turned, suddenly startled by the déjà vu sight of the waiter holding a tray of glasses. She held her breath as she looked for the movement past his shoulder. Out of the shadow behind a sheer sheet of white chiffon walked Zandra and her driver arm in arm.

Disappointed and a little tipsy, she lifted a glass from the tray, saluted them and returned her gaze to her dream man's portrait.

She paused with the glass half-way to her lips as the guests around her started to applaud. Her glass slipping from her fingertips as the image of his face moved closer. "Okay, that's enough wine for me, I'm obviously drunk," she berated herself.

She glanced at the floor where the broken glass scattered at her toes narrowly missing them but her dress hadn't been so lucky.

One minute she was counting her toes and the next, she was swept off her feet into big strong arms. "I'm fine, thank you, you can put me down..." Her words froze in her throat as she met the eyes of her painting, her dream man. She promptly fainted in his arms.

CHAPTER 22

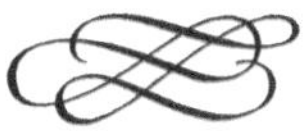

Morpheus quietly stole into the gallery. He'd been pacing nervously beside the car for the last hour.

He didn't feel normal in the human realm, his hands shook with fear. What if she rejected him? Finally, he couldn't wait any longer. He'd pulled the invitation out of his pocket and made his way to the entrance.

Once inside, he stayed in the shadows, until he saw her. Cheval Noland, his female, was the most magnificent thing he'd ever seen in all his very long existence. She stood there with a saddened expression on her beautiful face that tugged at his chest making it ache for her. He watched as a waiter tapped her shoulder and she turned, he stepped up behind her and waited.

His Chevi's eyes settled on him as she re-assumed her previous position, he saw her sway slightly as the glass slid from her hold, smashing on the timber floor around her exposed toes. Her focus was drawn to the splash marks soaking into her dress.

He took two large steps, further grinding the already crushed glass into the floor, as he swept her up in his arms, right where he honestly believed she belonged.

His protest falling on deaf ears, when her eyes met his, she fainted. He looked at Zandra, frantic for guidance. She ushered him toward the rear of the gallery, and out the back door. Stopping only briefly in their escape, Zandra spoke to some woman about Chevi not feeling well and they were taking her home.

He thought further on it as he nursed his beloved in the back seat of the limo, the entire sequence of events were tantamount to a kidnapping.

He held her closer as the car drove over

the bridge, he sighed, he was taking his woman home. His feelings for her overrode any inner conflict over what he was doing. He was taking her unconscious human form back to his realm.

CHEVI HAD ONLY BEEN OUT TO IT FOR A BRIEF few moments, but she kept herself limp, and her eyes closed. She was too embarrassed to return to the gallery full of people who had witnessed her untimely shock performance. She knew she was either in the strong embrace of her dream man or completely crazy.

She heard what was being said by Zandra to Olivia and was all too happy to just leave and get out of there. But now she was trying to figure out whether she was awake or dreaming. She wasn't game to lift her lids in case she found herself surrounded on the floor of the gallery. Chevi could no longer tell the difference between what was real and what wasn't.

She felt the warmth seep into her chilled

skin as she was positioned. She heard Zandra speak, alleviating some of her curiosity, "Sandy, I'll ride up front with Des, it'll give you more privacy. We should be home in about ten minutes."

He simply said, "Thank you, Zandra, for everything." The rumble of his chest as he spoke, the heat of his body and the sound of his voice, made Chevi's heart race.

Des had closed the door, then they were alone. She questioned whether to open her eyes or not.

AS THE VEHICLE REACHED HALF WAY HOME, Morpheus closed his eyes and tried to find Chevi in the dream world, unsure if his powers would work here in her world. Only he couldn't find her, finally he concluded that she was playing possum.

Well two could play that game, he leaned down close to Chevi's ear and growled just above a whisper, "You can open your beautiful brown eyes now, or I may have to put you over my knee and spank you for scaring me."

Chevi gasped, "You wouldn't?"

Morpheus chuckled, "This is my dream, I'll do what I want," then sucked her lobe between his warm lips, to prove his point.

Chevi shivered slightly as electricity zinged through her body connecting the sensation to her nipples making them bud. She wriggled a little in his lap as her pussy started to prepare for his touch.

Chevi didn't care at this point whether what was happening was real or a fabrication of her desperate mind. She was going along willingly for the ride, regardless. She'd figure the rest out later.

"I can't tell if this is real or not?" She placed her hand on his chest, she could feel the beat of his heart pounding under it.

"This is very real, you're real, I'm real, and this is really happening." He tried to reassure her as he kissed her deeply. The car pulled to a stop. Parked in front of a huge mansion, she heard doors opening and closing, then the rear door next to them opened.

The driver, holding Zandra's hand informed them, "You're on your own from here."

They both watched as Zandra and Destiny walked hand in hand into the gardens along the side of the driveway.

"Will you stay?" Morpheus eyed her warily, waiting for her answer.

How could she refuse such a plea, "Yes, but I don't know how long this dream is going to last."

Morpheus bundled her up and lifted her out of the limo. As he reached to close the door, she took his hand and said, "Wait, please." She gave him a smile, to indicate there wasn't anything to worry about, then waved her hand with concentration.

Nothing happened, it didn't work, she waved her hand again with determination, still nothing happened. "Oh my fucking god!" she exclaimed, gulping for air, "This is real, I'm not dreaming."

Morpheus laughed, "I assure you, this is indeed all very real." He swept her up into his arms and with one carefully placed foot, he kicked the door shut then strode into the house. When they reached the end of the hall, he asked Chevi to open the door. She turned the knob. They were surrounded by darkness for a moment, then she was being shifted. He took her hand and led her to the entry of his home.

Once inside, he pushed her exposed back to the cold timber, and took ownership of her lips. Her own parted to create a furious dance of tongues battling for dominance. She moaned into his mouth as his hands cupped her ass and lifted her to express his need to be inside her.

Thoughts ran through her head like what if the chemistry wasn't there in real life? What if? What if....? Her own body's need took over.

"If this isn't a dream, then how do I get you out of your clothes," she smirked, as their foreheads met allowing them to catch their breath.

"Any way we can," he lifted his hand and waved it over her dress, making it vanish. She reached down between them and unfastened his belt, then unzipped his fly.

"You don't play fair, Sandy," she gasped as she released his hardness, and using her legs to wrap around his waist, she pushed him between her slippery lips into her cave.

She bit his shoulder as he pounded her against the door. Hard and fast, long strokes taking them to heights they'd never been before.

"Who do you belong to?" he asked, holding her orgasm just out of reach, he needed to hear it.

"You Sandy, I belong to you. Always and forever." She screamed as his thumb found her swollen button about the place they joined.

"Then you'll stay, forever mine." He groaned as he spilled his love deep inside her pulsing pussy. "I love you." He whispered in her ear as the last of his seed surged. From some place in his mind, he pictured his seed buried in his female's womb, smaller than a grain of dream sand taking seed and swelling her body. He secretly craved it. He wasn't about to burst the sizzling connection between them by talking semantics.

CHAPTER 23

Morpheus carried his woman into the bathroom with his cock still buried deep. Every movement and sway of his hips had her whimpering with oohs or aargh's. His hardness returned in record time.

He had to think hard about why he'd brought her to this room. It seemed all the blood from his brain had moved south. South, that's right he wanted to wash her feet and make sure she hadn't been cut by the broken glass.

He turned and sat her ass on the basin bench. Kissed her intensely, then ever so slowly, slid himself free of her hot swollen glove.

"I need to see that you're not hurt," he commented as he lifted one foot for scrutiny. He gently removed the gold-colored sandal and tossed it in the bin next to the toilet. Satisfied there was no damage, he did the same with the other sandal.

Chevi leaned back to be as accommodating as possible, never before had she wanted a man so badly that she'd lost all her inhibitions. Opening her legs further to expose her womanly charms, she asked, "So, the things I saw and did with you in my dreams were kind of real too?"

His eyes fixed on her nakedness, "To me, they were as real as you are sitting there now, teasing me. Before you found me in your dreams, I didn't really exist, my desire for life was gone, and you brought me back from a very dark place. One I never want to see again. Can we get you cleaned up first, then we can talk. I can't think straight with you tempting me like this." He ran the back of his hand along her exposed slit coated in their combined release, his cock twitched with interest. So to avoid the immediate temptation, he turned to start the water in the shower, then returned to collect Chevi, before getting in.

He worshipped her curves, tracing all the beautiful colors inked on her skin, "One day, I want you to tell me about all these markings." As the water rinsed the suds away, his lips kissed them one by one. He licked, sucked and even grazed them with his teeth. An occasional nip here and there made Chevi curl her nails against the tiles.

After he was sure any shards of glass and remnants of champagne had been washed away, he towered over her from behind.

She eagerly pushed back into his body with a seductive invitation. Unable to resist her form of persuasion any longer, he held still as she pushed herself backwards to slowly swallow him whole, through her slippery folds.

"Fuck me, I'll never get enough of your tight pussy, I'm gonna stay buried inside you forever." Chevi had never gone in for dirty talk before, but his words were like a branding, he was marking her soul, claiming her as his, making her gush. He growled next to her ear, "That's it baby, cum for me, cum all over my cock," his hand circled her, his fingers wove their magical spell around and over her nub.

Chevi screamed, as her orgasm bit down hard, she came so hard she thought she was going to black out. He was right there with her, he hammered her contracting vault, finally spilling his seed so deep she could feel the throb of his heartbeat.

He collapsed against her exhausted body, the tiled wall the only thing offering them support. Chevi gasped for breath, "I...can't....breath," she panted.

"Sorry," he said, as he placed both hands on the wall and pushed himself off, sliding from her body.

Chevi stood with her cheek resting on the tiles, her legs too shaky to move. "Okay, I think I need to lay down for a bit."

"Me too," he agreed. One second, they were in the shower stall and next, they were snuggled up in his huge bed.

"What the hell," Chevi said as she lifted her head off his chest. "How did you do that?"

Morpheus explained, "This is my realm,

my home, my kingdom so to speak. I can make anything happen here," he lazily waved his hand around before settling back on Chevi's shoulder.

"I don't understand any of this, I'm trying, but I'm also struggling to figure out whether I'm awake or dreaming," Chevi sighed.

Morpheus decided the easiest way to explain everything was to show her, "Close your eyes for me," he asked as he laid her head back down on his chest. He gently placed two fingers on her temple and Chevi watched the story unfold behind her closed lids.

Everything somehow became clearer; she understood how she had manipulated his world in a fashion. The only way for them to be together was for him to enter her world and bring her into his.

He'd gone to extreme lengths to honor and please her; with Zandra's help he'd sent her the dress, the shoes, and the gems. Finally, a smile spread across her face, he'd even bought the entire collection of her paintings.

She got to keep her masterpiece if she chose to stay. There were images of things that had yet to pass as though he was asking with images what he couldn't put into words. A tear trickled from the corner of her eye. She finally understood her role in the grand picture of things. She was his counterweight, his balance, and he was hers, she was finally home, in this magical place in the arms of her god.

He patiently waited for her to respond, to say something. He was standing on the edge of a cliff, would she save him, or push him over into insanity?

Their eyes met, as she lifted her head to look at his face, the sincerity he displayed made her heart explode with love.

"I..." She was at a loss for words, "Yes," she kissed him tenderly then said what was in her heart and mind. "Yes, I'll stay, forever," she said, thinking dreams really do come true. They fell asleep in each other's arms into a dreamless sleep.

ABOUT THE AUTHOR

Melissa Bell is a USA Today Best Selling Author who lives in Brisbane, Australia. At a point in her life where she felt she needed something just for herself, she discovered the pleasures of writing. Her most frequently used comment to herself is there's not enough time in a day. She enjoys good food and good company, when she's not trying to concentrate on her writing. She also loves to laugh and most of the time, she cracks herself up. She is hoping that this is the start of something amazing and one day aspires to be listed amongst those blessed with the title of being on the New York Times Best Sellers list.

When she isn't writing she loves to read, many of which she has read over and over again while listening to her favorite Australian bands - Birds of Tokyo and Karnivool.

Please keep an eye out for other books by Melissa Bell.

Stay safe and thank you for reading my book.

ALSO BY MELISSA BELL

Please visit your favorite Book retailer to discover other books by Melissa Bell.

DUTIFUL GODS SERIES

Book #1 Destiny's Fate

Book#2 Taming Destruction

Book#3 Morpheus's Dream

Book #4 Defying Death

Book #5 Cosmo's Universe (TBA)

Five Brothers Series

Book#1 Houston
Book#2 Felan
Book#3 Tate
Book #4 Channon
Book #4.5 Lupe
(First story in 'Compilation'- A Collection
of Short Stories)
Book #5 London
Books still to come in this series include –
Blaez and Brody amongst others.
(So stay tuned)